MELVIN HOWARD'S

FIRESIDE CHATS

BY
MICHAEL T. KRIEGER

Dedicated to the students of Rossford High School

Special thanks to Gail Mann of Elmore Publishing, and to Marvin Anderson and Gary Blakeman for computer assistance.

Cover art work by Tiffany A. Mills, 1992.

I

When I was young I was like most children in behavior and attitude, but I appeared fragile since God had graced me with every known form of allergy, plus poor eyesight, and incoordination. Despite my seemingly countless deficiencies, a vivid imagination was my gift. Because of my imagination, I was an avid reader and highly prone to daydreaming. Adventures were my favorites and through daydreaming I heroically took the place of the characters I had continuously read about. So many times I carried out Robin Hood's deeds for him, or took my place in the saddle of the Connecticut Yankee, or sought to harpoon the mighty Moby Dick. While these travels occasionally got in the way of my grades, they really only hindered me when it came to socializing with others. Since I didn't pay attention to my school work, I was labeled as being dumb. This inattentiveness mixed with my inability to be athletic like the other boys kept me safely in my own quiet corner. By myself I never had to impress anyone else, nor did I have to become uncomfortable about meeting others.

Nevertheless everyone needs interaction with other human beings, and often this interaction can lead to deep friendship. Just such a surprising incident happened to me in the fall shortly after I had entered the seventh grade.

On a cold, rainy day in late October I was strenuously peddling my father's bike toward home after school. The bike was big and clumsy with tractor-size tires, a rusty wire basket in front, and a rickety chain that always fell off. Struggling with the bike and my lack of coordination made my short journey home virtually an impossible endeavor.

The road I travelled is just like roads in most small towns throughout the country with small post-World War II homes, picket fences, and neatly trimmed lawns on one side and a wide-open field lined with telephone poles and mailboxes on the other side. Unfortunately the road is also narrow and poorly cared for by the county, so it has its share of potholes along its edges. On this day in October the rain made it extra difficult to maneuver the bike around the potholes. For the most part, I was going to make it all right, but I decided that the going would be easier if I stayed on the road itself. I was right until a car sped in behind me. I had to get out of the road, but my only alternative was to ride straight into a canyon-size pothole. Not wishing to bounce off the car's bumper, I tried to guide the crippled bike through a tiny patch of gravel between the road and the pothole. When the bike's front wheel hit the gravel it did not handle the transition in terrain well, and it slid, throwing me from its saddle as if it were a bucking bronco. I fell spread-eagle into the mud just past the potholes. I lay there stupefied, dazed, and feeling hatred for the bike that had once again defied me.

Then, to add to my growing humiliation the car screeched to a stop, the door opened, and the driver catapulted from the vehicle, his eyes wild with fear. He was an older man of stocky build, and he was wearing a yellow raincoat with no hat. In the flash he was next to me, kneeling beside me and staring intently at my muddy face. For a split second, I had visions of this man abducting me, and whisking me off to some bizarre foreign prison where I would be tortured until I revealed any secrets I knew about the United States' inter-political workings. Heroically, in that same instant, I decided I wouldn't tell no matter what. I would preserve my patriotism even if they threatened me with the lives of my loved ones. I wouldn't talk. I had to be mentally tough.

Instead of doing great harm to me he spoke: "Are you all right? Are you hurt?"

Immediately I did not know how to answer since I could not answer both questions with one word. Instead, I tried to get up, hopefully answering both of the stranger's questions. Once up, however, there were two problems: my bike was broken and my clothing was filthy and damp.

"Well, your bike is in desperate need of repairs. I think I've got the proper tools at my house. Do you live far?"

"No," I answered.

I stood before him helpless and drenched. But, even though I felt helpless, I was at ease, for this old man had a sort of trustworthiness about him, almost like my grandfather. In fact, I was sure that they might be similar in age.

"Well, why don't you hop in, and I'll take you to my house. We'll stoke up the fire, and get you a change of clothes. My son's old clothes just might do for awhile till we can get your own clothes dry." He spoke these words with caring and warmth. It was not hard to tell that this man meant well and was not an international spy or terrorist.

"When we get to my place we'll call your folks to let them know you are all right," he said as I slid into the front seat.

The old car rattled and shook as if it needed a new muffler, but otherwise, it ran well. The car's interior smelled of cigar smoke and aged rubber. The car also needed shocks, for any bump caused the auto to bounce wildly as if we were perched on the hump of a camel.

The old man awkwardly maneuvered the old car around a sharp corner.

The car slightly reminded me of my father's bike that had just tossed me into the mud only moments ago. Apparently his house wasn't far, for he moved up closer to the windshield, maybe to get a better look. He began tapping the brake to slow the lumbering relic. He flipped on his directional and turned the wheel as if it were the wheel to a giant ship, and safely guided the car into a stone driveway in front of a neatly-kept, old Victorian-style house. The beautiful home told me right away that this old man knew how to live. The lawn and the bushes were trimmed nicely. In the middle of the yard was a bird bath. During my momentary observation, a sparrow landed to bathe. In the same instant, I felt this was bizarre because it was still raining, and birds generally do not make it a habit to fly about in foul weather.

During this time the friendly old man had lifted my bike from the car and had carried it into the garage. Easily he laid it down on the floor, apparently so he wouldn't hurt it anymore than it had already been.

"Let's get you inside so you can change clothes," he said. His voice was low and easy, and it gently roused me from my dreamlike observation of the sparrow. His voice reminded me of my mother's gentle rubbing of my shoulder to wake me from my naps when I was very young; or the time I drifted asleep last weekend while watching the late show. His voice sounded of warmth and love. It did not boom, but instead, his voice sounded fluffy like a pillow and as gentle as the rain splashing my cheeks.

He opened the door to his home for me with a smile and gesture of his hand, "Welcome sir, to my most humble home," he said with pride ripping through every pore of his body. There was something else about him which I wasn't quite sure of yet.

The inside wasn't near as conservative as the outside. His living room was giant with very plush shag carpeting, a small piano, drab olive drapes. The ceiling was very short. This made the room appear long and squashed. The kitchen was a cheery yellow with white tile floor and randomly placed green throw rugs. The kitchen was flanked by a casual family room. It was equipped with a twenty-four inch color console TV with a remote control module sitting atop a pile of newspapers that were strewn across a garage sale coffee table. In one corner was a recliner that had big, puffy cushions. Next to the recliner there was a well-varnished oak end table with an ashtray overflowing with peanut shells. Beside that was another ashtray that was permanently dusty and gray from cigar ashes. The one unique thing about the family room was the mounted fish on the paneled wall above the television. The fish was gigantic and looked so plastic from the effects of the taxidermist that it seemed impossible that it actually ever lived.

"That's a blue marlin. I caught it myself on a fishing trip in the Caribbean."

"You caught this? It's so big!" Finally my exasperation had subsided and I was able to speak.

He went on: "Yep, I caught it myself. It was the first time I ever tried to catch a deep sea fish too. I was told at one time it was a record, but I never had it recorded."

3

As he finished the last word he handed me a red and black checked flannel shirt and a pair of rumpled blue corduroys.

"Here, these should keep you warm for awhile," he said. The old man then directed me toward a bathroom where I could change.

Instinctively, I shed my wet clothing and put on these temporary hand-me-downs. The old man was right, the clothes did fit, and most of all, they were warm and comfortable. While I dressed, the old man had tossed a log into the fireplace and had set about starting a fire. Instantly, the spark from the match took hold of the crumpled newspapers and burst into a brilliant, orange flame. The man crouched in front of the small fire watching it grow for a short time as if it were a living thing that he might nurse to maturity until it could maintain itself. I watched as the glow from the flame grew and slowly erased the shadows on the old man's face. As the flame flickered the warmth grew within the room and forced me to forget that just thirty minutes ago I was soaked to the skin in cold, muddy water.

"So, what is your name?" The old man said as he gazed into the fire.

Slowly and carefully I answered. "Martin Hovrick," I replied, clearing my throat.

"It is good to meet you, Martin," responded the old man with a smile, the reflection of the fire's glow in his soothing hazel eyes. "My name is," he continued with an air of nobility, "Melvin Howard."

"It's nice to meet you too, sir," I said shakily. For some reason the name did not fit him. 'Melvin Howard' seemed just too regular. Already the old man seemed to express an unexplainable uniqueness that definitely deserved a better title than 'Melvin Howard'.

"What is your phone number so I can call your folks?"

Once again, I responded straight forward, "893-1564."

He murmured the number to himself a couple times before he plopped into the recliner. He pushed through the peanut shells scattered about the end table and produced an old-fashioned telephone. The telephone seemed to fit the room appropriately for it was an old, black upright phone with the receiver being a separate attachment only connected by a rubber wire. Melvin Howard briskly dialed the antique, which was in perfect working order.

"You know?...", he suddenly stopped in mid-sentence, "Hello, Mrs. Hovrick?"

Pause.

"My name is Melvin Howard, and I live up the road from you a bit. The reason I am calling is to let you know that Martin will be late."

A longer pause.

"No, no, he is all right. He fell off his bicycle into some muddy water."

Brief pause.

"Yes, that's right, and it was a bit of my fault because I was driving a little reckless..."

Pause.

4

"No, ma'am, I didn't run over him. I merely forced him off the road by accident."

Long pause.

"My intentions are good I assure you. After his bicycle is fixed and his clothes are dry I will bring him home directly, in perhaps, an hour."

Pause again.

"O.K. No, really, that's all right. My reaction would be the same. Just one moment."

Then Melvin Howard dropped the receiver from his ear, covered it with his hand, and turned to face me.

"She wants to speak to you," he said passively.

I took the phone from him. Even though I felt awkward with the antique, I managed to get the receiver up to my ear and speak into it.

"Mom?"

My mother was a good lady, although a bit over-protective at times. She was probably worried that I was being kidnapped by Melvin Howard. Quite obviously, she is the root to much of my over-active imagination.

"Yes, I'm fine. He seems to be very nice," I said reassuringly.

"I want you home soon, Martin. Make sure he brings you directly home, or I will send your father to get you. Is that understood?". She was definitely concerned. The sound of my voice was not enough to convince her of my safety.

"Yes Mom. I'll be home as soon as my clothes are dry."

With that we exchanged our good-byes and hung up.

I turned from the phone to see an intent look upon my host's face. Embarrassedly, I smirked a feeble grin in his direction.

"She doesn't trust me, does she?", said Melvin Howard flatly.

My instincts told me he was hurt by the reaction to mother's concern on the phone.

"She's nice enough, and I love her but I'm all she and Dad have so they worry, I guess," I replied hoping to return some of that flare that he had previously shone in his eyes.

"You know, it was different when I was your age."

"Was it?", I stammered for I wondered what exactly he was trying to say.

"I'm seventy-years-old in your book. But, in my book I'm seventy-years-young! You see it's all in the way you look at the world."

I was still confused.

"You see I have been lucky enough to live a very full life, and my only goal is to let my life get more full," he continued philosophically. He was beginning to sound like my grandfather; however, there was still something quite different about Melvin Howard. First of all, he didn't look seventy. Secondly, he seemed to have something to say on this topic of old age. His whole outlook on aging must be vastly different than every other old man I had ever met because he was so fit for his age. With this quick thought, I decided to listen closely to him. His words were careful and mesmerizing as he told about himself. The conversation, only moments ago had been just small talk, and now Melvin Howard gave a sample of his thoughts like he was showing me slides from a recent camping trip to the Wisconsin Dells.

"That's nice," he continued, "that your mom cares so much about you, that she needs to watch out for you; but when I was your age you didn't worry about strangers and violence. People felt safe. People were really free. The problem is people started to abuse their freedom by suddenly including harassing other folks into their own definition of freedom."

He was right. When I was in kindergarten I walked to school freely. But, now because I was a social outcast, I often didn't feel as free or comfortable walking or riding my clumsy bicycle home because there was always the possibility that I would turn into the topic of ridicule for some group of students whose only saving grace was their popularity. "Because too many folks allowed their freedom to get out of control, laws had to be enforced," Melvin Howard spoke these last words as if he were narrating a long story because he stopped for a very effective pause. The fire flickered and popped as a flood of warmth engulfed the room filling me with warmth and a certain fulfillment, or peace - that was it! This overwhelming feeling of peace that now circulated in me, I had never felt before, yet I had scarcely met this man. The fire's warmth seemed to enter my pores, prickle my hair, and race feverishly in my blood. Little did he know, but Melvin Howard was introducing me to, what would be my first twinges of true friendship.

"Don't get me wrong," he continued. "There were always laws, but in those days people respected the laws, as well as each other."

"Why did things change?" I asked.

He continue with all the finesse of a knowledgeable professor, "People became too smart." He made it seem simple. "When I was younger than I am now we didn't know about many of the bad things that people did to others because the information wasn't available. If there was anybody that was interested in these bad things they were made an instant enemy of the entire society."

"Then what?," I asked curiosity welling inside me.

"Oh, they were severely punished and the strictness of the punishment obviously depended upon the crime committed."

We sat quietly for a moment. My eyes studied his face still trying to figure out what was so impressive about this man, Melvin Howard. His eyes, at the moment, seemed distant, yet clear like a northern lake. The flames danced in both of his pupils. The fire at that moment seemed incredibly, but comfortably, warm as if it were pouring from within him. His eyes were lost in the fire. He watched it as if it talked to him; and then trancelike, he began to speak what would become the first word of the first story Melvin Howard ever told me, of which the string would be long. Neither of us realized at the time that we were both about to embark upon a journey that would bind us closely and permanently as friends.

"I do remember when I was thirteen-years-old, and I was living with my family in a rural community over in Henry County...

II

The thirteen-year-old boy named Melvin slowly walked down the beaten path toward the small school. It was a long walk, but he never really minded except during January when winter's coldest winds came tearing across the countryside as sharp as razors, cutting through every thing that stood in its way. But, today was warm, and the time of year was fall. The trees were beautiful this time of year, and the young, but observant Melvin felt lucky that there were several maples that lined the path along his route every morning. The leaves were a collage of brilliant reds and sunny yellows that added integrity and spice to an otherwise exhausting flat stretch of fields.

To the average traveller or onlooker there wasn't much to see; but to Melvin Howard his walk down the path every morning was like a journey into places unknown. He made it a point to look for something pleasantly different every day. At thirteen he was very observant and had a knack for discovering hidden, intrinsic beauty in nearly everything. Today his fascination was with a peculiar maple branch he had found along the road. The branch was shaped exactly like a "Y" and it was as thick as his thumb.

'What a marvelous thing,' he thought to himself. Nature's creations always intrigued him, especially nature's imperfections. This branch was just such an imperfection. Because it wasn't like the other branches, it took on a certain speciality for the boy, who vowed that because of its uniqueness the branch justly deserved to be used for something important. Misfits never bothered Melvin Howard because he always believed that what his grandfather had said was true. He had said, 'Melvin, you've got to appreciate anything that is different because if God took the time to make it different there is obviously something very special about it. And, when you see what is different about everyone and everything you will be able to treat them special.'

The maple branch was a misfit because it wasn't like the other branches, but that made it safe for Melvin to apply his grandfather's philosophy for there was a uniqueness about everything, including the branch. While his

8

walk to school continued he began to think for what the Y-shaped branch could be used. Suddenly, his thoughts struck gold. It was easy! He would make a slingshot and he would use crabapples for ammunition to shoot at targets. Immediately the boy was excited, and he couldn't wait until the end of the day so he could begin work on his slingshot. With his adrenaline flowing, Melvin Howard raced the last remaining half mile to school. Before he entered the school, however, he realized that he could not bring the branch inside because that might invoke a slew of questioning from his teacher, Mrs. Grable. So, quickly, he found a convenient spot to hide his new-found toy. He tucked it beneath the hedges in front of the school, where he was sure the branch would still be at the end of the day.

The school day dragged for Melvin Howard as he found it exhausting to add fractions, diagram sentences, and to read about the change of the seasons when his attention was sufficiently diverted to the type of slingshot he would make. He pictured himself loading the rawhide strap with a crabapple, focusing on a tin can perched up on a fence post about ten yards away, and finally shooting the tin can off the fence. He smiled jubilantly, and unknowingly, he sighed aloud. The boy in front of him, Buddy Crowel, heard the sigh, which indicated a daydream in action, something that Buddy was probably quite good at recognizing, for he was often gripped in a daydream himself. Unfortunately for Buddy, he had to occasionally tell the class about his daydreams as a punishment because he was so easily distracted from his lessons.

"What ya thinkin' about, Melvin?", Buddy slyly whispered over his right shoulder.

Melvin quickly returned from his trance at the sound of Buddy's voice. Cautiously, Melvin waited for Mrs. Grable to begin writing on the chalkboard once again before he spoke to Buddy. Mrs. Grable was asking Susan Parker, the smartest student in the class, and the ugliest girl in class, a question about the summer months and how these months are not the same in the southern hemisphere. Susan correctly said 'that in the southern hemisphere winter is experienced, while the summer is experienced by the northern hemisphere.' After her answer Mrs. Grable, once again, turned to the chalkboard.

Leaning slightly forward in his seat, Melvin said, "Hey Buddy, I'm making a slingshot after school tonight."

"Really," responded Buddy in a whisper.

Melvin and Buddy weren't the best of friends, but they weren't enemies either, and at times they even hung around together during recess.

"Yeah," whispered Melvin Howard as Mrs. Grable again turned to write on the board.

Buddy half-turned in his seat and said that he used to have a slingshot but he lost it last weekend when he and his cousin went fishing for bullhead in the Blanchard River. Apparently, he had spoken too loud though because Mrs. Grable quickly pivoted, tapped the chalk against the board impatiently, then sternly asked Buddy to quit "the idle chatter" and to "face front". Buddy

9

was usually very good at gaining Mrs. Grable's distrust. He was not a good student, but he was a consistent troublemaker. This time, Buddy did as he was told while several of the others snickered at him for his irresponsibility.

"Buddy, I want you to explain to the class what you were talking to Melvin about," said Mrs. Grable flatly.

Buddy got quickly to his feet, stammered an apology, and then he informed the whole class that Melvin was going to make a slingshot after school.

"Is this true Melvin?," interrogated Mrs. Grable.

Melvin Howard also, quickly jumped to his feet. "Yes ma'am, it is true, and I am very sorry for disturbing the class," he answered with his voice wavering from embarrassment because the class was now laughing at him as well as Buddy Crowel. Both boys stood before the class with their faces flushed crimson as if they were being persecuted by one of the country's highest courts.

Mrs. Grable spoke again. Her voice never faltered nor changed an octave for more emphasis. She didn't need more emphasis because she would get her point across effectively without even speaking another word.

"Boys, come up to my desk please."

She gave this order and reached for the switch she kept on the chalk tray for just such an emergency. Neither boy spoke, but respectfully took his place alongside Mrs. Grable's desk. The switch fell swiftly across the buttocks of each boy, but both of them handled their punishment like men by gritting their teeth. After all, there was always plenty of time during recess to wince like boys.

That afternoon during recess Buddy and Melvin met to talk more about the slingshot; a conversation, which came about mostly due to Buddy's insistence and overwhelming curiosity. So, reluctantly, Melvin Howard took Buddy Crowel to the hedges in front of the school to show him the branch he intended to use for the slingshot. Buddy took the branch from Melvin and looked it over closely.

Buddy agreed, "This is a fine branch for a slingshot, Melvin. I'd really like to see it when its all finished."

Thoughtlessly, Melvin said, "Really? I'll bring it to school tomorrow." Both boys were too caught up in the talk ahead that they had failed to remember that bringing slingshots or weapons to school was not permitted and the punishment for breaking this rule was stiff. Anyone that broke this rule usually got suspended from school for five days. This wasn't good because then the student responsible had to have his parents involved.

That night, after school, and after his chores were completed Melvin Howard set to work with a pocket knife, a square of sandpaper, a rubber band, and a rawhide patch, which he bought for five cents after school at the local drugstore. First, he carefully wittled the bark off of the unique branch. Beneath the branch's weathered silver-gray covering was a soft tan wood that was dry enough so the sanding was easy. After the branch was smoothed perfectly and even rubbed white in spots, Melvin Howard used his pocket knife to chisel two small holes, one in each tip of the "Y". He then slid the rubber band through the rawhide and securely strapped the rubber band through the holes. The rubber band was in place, and with some minor adjustments, Melvin Howard made the band extra taught. Finally, on the back of the slingshot he carved his initials intricately. It was truly a work of art. Now, all that had to be done was to see how effective it was. He placed a small pebble in the rawhide strap, raised the slingshot, squared up, and fired for a small space on the side of his family's barn. He was at better then twenty paces when he sent the pebble ricochetting off the barn. The small stone struck the wood solidly and left a sizeable knick. Melvin Howard inspected the knick with his finger and smiled. The slingshot was perfect. Not only did it look nice, but it had an accurate shot too. He felt surprisingly successful and even a little cocky. Buddy Crowel would be impressed, and Melvin could hardly wait to show the slingshot to him the next day at school.

It was incredible how something so basic, he thought, could be turned into something so creative and potentially useful. Melvin had taken something as simple as a fallen maple branch and converted it into a virtual work of art that could be used tirelessly by him in his free time. He felt wonderful and glad that he was observant enough to realize the uniqueness within the branch.

The next day at school Melvin informed Buddy that he would show the slingshot to him during recess. Both boys were fidgety, but quiet through the morning. Melvin could hardly wait to show off the slingshot, for in his whole life he had never been so proud of something. He had very creatively converted one of nature's most unique creations, he felt, into something that could even hold Buddy Crowel's attention.

Finally, Mrs. Grable dismissed the class for lunch and recess. Buddy sprinted ahead of the rest of the class and waited for Melvin who was not far behind. Buddy was noticeably impatient, and upon realizing this, Melvin decided to act cocky.

"Where's the slingshot at?" asked Buddy with curiosity oozing from every word he uttered.

"I've got it," started Melvin with arrogance. "I'm not sure I can let you see it though."

"How come?!" screamed Buddy. He appeared to be insulted by Melvin's suggestion of secrecy.

"What makes you so sure you can be trusted? I mean, this is a pretty nice slingshot," continued Melvin.

"C'mon!" shouted Buddy.

"Well," Buddy was wincing with anticipation and even Melvin couldn't allow himself to tease Buddy any longer. "I'll let you see it on one condition," urged Melvin secretly.

"Sure. C'mon Melvin, quit playin' around!" Buddy was, indeed impatient.

"O.K., let's go. It's over here." Melvin gestured with a wave of his arm toward the same set of hedges as he had stashed the branch in the day before. Buddy's eyes lighted up and he smiled. To himself, Melvin hoped that Buddy wouldn't be jealous and try to take advantage of his own good nature. He had heard that Buddy Crowel could be like that from some of the other boys at school. They walked over to the hedges, and Melvin ducked inside of them quickly. When he popped back out he held the beautifully crafted slingshot. He presented it to Buddy who grabbed it greedily for a closer look. The slingshot was finished and smooth, yet the carving and sanding that Melvin had done to it had not weakened the wood in the least. Buddy pulled on the band loosely at first, then with more force. Melvin was not worried. He knew that the slingshot was sound so it did not matter how much tugging Buddy did.

"How does it shoot?," asked the inquisitive Buddy.

"I was about ten yards from the barn yesterday and I put some deep knicks in it with stones." Melvin chose to be truthful since he couldn't come up with a convincing exaggeration. No matter, Buddy seemed convinced. Melvin glowed with pride as he watched Buddy feign firing the slingshot. Actually, he wasn't sure why it was so important to him that Buddy be impressed by the slingshot. Buddy, after all, was nobody special, just another typical kid at school. Yet, Melvin cared about Buddy's opinion on the slingshot as if Buddy were the world's greatest critic and expert on slingshot construction. There was some social test here; or perhaps, some new, even stronger sense of acceptance because, for now, Melvin appeared in Buddy's eyes as not just any other kid at school. In fact, it could be safe to say that Melvin in an acute sense had established a strong feeling of respect from Buddy; which, he was sure, Buddy would ultimately transfer to the other boys.

"Can I try it?," Buddy asked, shaking him from his intent gaze.

"Sure, but let me go first," smiled Melvin. He really felt as though he had accomplished something big.

Buddy obediently handed the slingshot to Melvin who loaded the rawhide strap with a crab apple.

"What should I shoot at?," asked Melvin cockily.

Buddy's eyes wandered about the playground for a couple seconds indecisively. Finally, "How 'bout that old tree over there?" Buddy was pointing at an old elm tree about twenty-five yards away.

Melvin shrugged and raised the slingshot in front of him. He aimed at the tree with the rubber band pulled taught. With a quick wrist flick the band snapped forward, which sent the crab apple zinging through the air until it splatted solidly against the tree and bounced off as a piece of squashed rind and juice.

"Wow!" exclaimed Buddy.

The slingshot was even stronger than Melvin had expected. Now Buddy simply could not wait to try it himself. Without hesitation, Melvin handed the slingshot over to Buddy, who quickly loaded it with a crab apple and aimed at the same tree. The crab apple Buddy fired was equally as accurate as the previous one, for it too smacked solid against the trunk of the old elm. "This thing really shoots well!" shouted Buddy excitedly.

Melvin remained speechless in light of his new accomplishment, instead he took the slingshot back from Buddy and loaded it again. The two boys spent the next ten minutes trading shots with the slingshot. Both of them fired twenty shots each at the tree and kept score for ever crab apple that connected with the tree. Melvin won the contest 15-12. After the game, however, neither boy had tired of the slingshot, but both had grown tired of the target. The tree was definitely too easy now, and since they both felt proficient in hitting it, they decided to look for a new target. Buddy suggested that they try a moving target because that would be challenging, plus it would be different every time they played. Melvin was hesitant because knowing Buddy he was probably thinking about birds, and shooting animals as defenseless as a bird always bothered Melvin.

What do ya have in mind, Buddy?," asked Melvin, almost wishing he hadn't asked.

"I was thinking," Buddy began. He had a cruel little smirk on his face. Obviously, his troublesome mind was conjuring something devilish.

"What about one of the girls?," asked Buddy with a flare of the same arrogance that Melvin had been recently possessed with since the construction of the slingshot.

"I'm not so sure Buddy," said Melvin feebly; but it was too late because Buddy did not hear him. Buddy was already creeping across the playground with Melvin's slingshot in hand. Since Melvin couldn't bear to lose the slingshot he had worked so hard on, he found he had no choice but to follow. Besides, he was intrigued by whom Buddy intended on shooting, even if it wasn't such a good idea.

Buddy continued to sneak through the playground, every now and then dropping to all fours as if he were involved in war maneuvers behind enemy lines. Melvin did his best to hang closely with Buddy, but the course that was chosen did not seem to be premeditated. The boys crept sneakily, but recklessly to where some of the girls were playing. Here they ducked behind a tree out of sight of the oblivious girls. Cleverly and intently, Buddy loaded the slingshot with a crab apple and stepped out from behind the tree. Apparently, this mission belonged to Buddy, and nobody could change that. His eye was keen, his arms were rigid and tight, and his fingers were nimble and ready to give the rubber band the last strumming it needed to send the crab apple airborne into the circle of innocent girls. Suddenly, Buddy's fingers opened and let the band fly. The crab apple traveled the necessary distance and lofted into the girls' circle. Buddy's shot, as Melvin had originally thought, was not a haphazard one, but rather perfectly gauged and distinctly designated for none other than Susan Parker. The crab apple landed squarely on the bridge of Susan's nose and squished juice all over her glasses. Susan screamed bloody murder, the other girls scattered, Buddy raised his arms in triumph, and Melvin slumped down behind the tree trying to suppress the inevitable giggle that was already starting to snort from his nostrils. Finally he gave in to his laughter and keeled over holding his stomach spasmodically until tears flowed from his eyes. Meanwhile, Buddy re-loaded the slingshot in order to take another potshot at one of the other girls who was now definitely moving; just as Buddy had predicted. Now, he had Sylvia Myers in his sights. Once again, Buddy let the crab apple fly. This time he "beaned" Sylvia square in the middle of the back. She shrieked an ear-shattering scream and quickly dashed into the school.

Buddy snickered and re-loaded while Melvin just rolled in the grass laughing, failing to notice that Mrs. Grable came out of the school led by a hysterical Sylvia. Buddy Crowel once again had the slingshot arched and loaded. This time, however, because of his snickering his aim was careless, and the crab apple sailed right at Mrs. Grable. The boys realized all too late what was going to happen because before they knew it Mrs. Grable took the crab apple right in the middle of her forehead. Mrs. Grable screamed both out of fright and disgust. Buddy and Melvin were speechless. They just sat behind the tree with their mouths wide open and their eyes popping out like neon signs. What could they do? They could not run for it was far too late for that. They couldn't apologize by saying it was an accident just because they intended to hit one of the girls and not their teacher. Groveling on their hands and knees for forgiveness seemed to be too humiliating, but still it was the only realistic solution.

Regardless, it was too late. Mrs. Grable had come marching like an army general toward the tree where the boys were trying to hide. She was so mad she was huffing like an old steam engine. It was amazing that her glasses did not get fogged up. Buddy was frozen and lifeless. Melvin thought about running away, after all it was Buddy who shot the crab apple, and he knew he could out run Mrs. Grable. Melvin, however, remained an accomplice as long as he remained by the tree. How could he be held as responsible as Buddy, since all he really did was make the slingshot? That would be just like saying that Smith and Wesson were actually to blame for all the deaths caused by their weapons.

It was too late for thought-provoking analogies because Mrs. Grable was already swooping down on them like a giant condor. She looked as if she would take no prisoners. Life had been the best thirteen years that Melvin Howard could have ever hoped for; but now it was coming to a fast but painful end at the hands of this crazed teacher. Didn't she realize that God was a forgiving god?

Strongly, Mrs. Grable seized both boys by their shirt collars and easily hoisted them to their feet. Melvin realized that her grip was inescapable as terror washed through his body. He had never been in serious trouble with Mrs. Grable before. Even Buddy who was always in trouble for something was scared. It was plain to see, the fun and games had ended. Mrs. Grable dragged both boys back across the yard and into the school. She would waste

14

no time.

"Boys, I am utterly appalled at you behavior!" shouted Mrs. Grable. "Not only have you teased and harassed the other students, but you have blatantly shown disrespect for me." Mrs. Grable paused briefly because of exasperation. "Furthermore," she continued, "you are both aware of the rule we have regarding slingshots at school!"

That was true. Slingshots were illegal at school because they could often lead students to participate in ill-advised behavior, for which, Melvin and Buddy now stood as prime examples. This rule was not to be broken at Mrs. Grable's school. She was a strict disciplinarian and a firm believer in the philosophy that the justice carried out should serve the crime committed. The slingshot incident for which Melvin and Buddy were responsible was definitely a serious crime, and they were convinced Mrs. Grable would not make any exceptions.

Without further adieu, Mrs. Grable reached for the switch on the chalk tray. She poised like a leopard, and the stare that fixed her eyes on the two juvenile delinquents was forty below zero.

The switch rose and fell on the buttocks of each boy five times. The swats were hard and relentless that seared life-long branded lessons into the bottoms of both Melvin and Buddy. The ferocity with which they were stung by the switch made it impossible not to cry. With each new crack that the switch beat into Melvin and Buddy, there seemed to be a river of tears and sobs squeezed out of them. Crying was the only thing that could ease the pain, but it really did not cover it up that well.

Mrs. Grable finally put the switch back on the chalk tray and began writing furiously. She was obviously still angry. Finally, she handed a note to each boy that was to go to each of their parents.

"Both of you are dismissed from school for now. Beginning tomorrow you both will be suspended for five days at which time you will receive failing grades for any of the lessons you miss," Mrs. Grable said sternly.

The gavel had fallen and nothing could undo the situation that Buddy and Melvin had created for themselves. Melvin realized, even at this young age that the worst part of the punishment was that he would fail any of the assignments that he missed. He felt like a condemned criminal. None of this would have happened if he hadn't felt the need to impress Buddy Crowel. In two days Melvin and Buddy had gotten in trouble at school twice when Melvin had never really been in trouble before. For the first time Melvin was being judged by the company he kept. He did not like being stereotyped with Buddy Crowel, and he hated Buddy for helping him get into trouble. Most of all, he hated himself for the lack of trust he had started to create for himself in Mrs. Grable's eyes.

As the two boys walked slowly and humbly into the playground again Buddy sniffed his nose. "My dad is goin' to kill me when he finds out."

"Mine too," remarked Melvin soberly. His parents punishing him seemed to be the least of his worries, however.

"Hey, Melvin, why don't we just not tell our parents. And every day when we're supposed to be at school we'll go hiking or fishing or something?," said Buddy with a twinkle of joy rekindling in his empty-looking eyes. Buddy really was dumb and his plan made even less sense than shooting the girls with the slingshot. No, he was already in enough trouble, Melvin decided, and Buddy was worthless for a friend. So, with no notice to Buddy, Melvin burst into a run. He ran for home. He wanted to be honest with his folks, and he wanted to leave Buddy behind. He couldn't run from his troubles, but he certainly could run from Buddy.

III

"That day I ran all the way home," said Melvin Howard, coughing back a quick but hearty laugh. "My dad whipped me so hard I could've melted a block of ice just by sitting on it."

I found the story enjoyable and even humorous, and this heart-warming tale added to the already comfortable clothes and fire. Unfortunately, dusk was slowly creeping in through the one shaded window in Melvin Howard's family room. The growing darkness added brilliance to the fire and even a bit more serenity to this humble but homey occasion. I could not decide if it was right to feel this comfortable around a stranger that I had only met about an hour ago. I wanted to listen more to Melvin Howard to see if he knew any other entertaining stories about his own childhood; but the next words from his mouth came suddenly, "Mercy! It's getting late. Your folks will worry."

He quickly got up from his Lazy Boy and left the room. He returned with my clothes, only this time they were dry. Melvin Howard left the room while I quickly changed. I handed back the old clothes that he had provided for me and for some reason, I still wished that I was wearing them.

"I feel sort of bad, Martin," the old man said softly. His eyes were not twinkling now.

"Why?" I asked confused.

"The whole time I was sitting here gabbing, I should have been fixing your bike and now it's time for you to go," he said noticeably disappointed in himself.

"I really don't mind," I said without much expression. "I loved the story, thanks."

"That's all right," he replied, "but you got to watch me because I'll get to talkin' and completely forget about everything else."

He helped me with my coat, and we both walked out to the old car that was napping in the garage from what seemed like a strenuous drive earlier.

"Tell you what!" exclaimed Melvin Howard, "I'll fix your bike tonight and bring it to you first thing in the morning."

It seemed like a good idea to me too, so I agreed. Since tomorrow was Saturday I would not need the bike early in the morning to go to school.

"How about if I bring the bike around about noon tomorrow?"

"Sure," I shrugged.

"Good," he said. "We've disturbed your folks enough for today."

The next day about noon Melvin Howard was there knocking lightly on my front door with the bike beside him; however, it didn't look exactly like the same bike that had tossed me into a mud puddle just yesterday afternoon. Melvin Howard was definitely a man of his word. He said that he would fix the bike, but he had practically re-built the bike instead. Not only did he fix the chain that was constantly a nuisance, but he had replaced it entirely and oiled it. The hulking tires that added to the bike's clumsiness were replaced with smaller, thinner ones with rough, new tread. The spokes and rims and handle bars were shined up so that they gleamed in the early morning sunshine. He had taken the basket off and replaced it with a headlight and an odometer, but on the back, behind the seat, was a small pouch for carrying items, which sufficiently replaced the ridiculous basket.

"This is really great!" I exclaimed.

Melvin Howard smiled a mile wide and insisted that his efforts were really nothing. No matter how modest he was I could not stop thanking him.

"It was the least I could do after running you off the road and getting you home so late last night," answered Melvin Howard.

"Please come inside," I said eagerly.

My folks would be shocked too, and I couldn't wait to show the bike to them. Melvin Howard had met them last night, which was the only assurance they needed to cancel out any misconceptions that they might have had about this man and his intentions. My father was impressed by the man's intellect and honesty, while my mom felt that Melvin Howard was charming and gentlemanly. Surely, after they saw the bike and how he had improved it they would be grateful enough to invite him to have brunch with us. Brunch was a Saturday morning tradition in our family, and my mom was a marvelous cook.

As predicted, my parents were, at first, stunned at the appearance of the bike and the reasons an old man might have for rebuilding the "old junker"; then they were delighted. Melvin Howard had truly won my entire family over, and naturally, my mother suggested that he stay for brunch for all of his troubles.

"Now, that's not really necessary folks. I was the one who owed the favor," said Melvin Howard with insurmountable modesty.

But, my mother was never one to take no for an answer, especially when she was offering her cooking.

"Nonsense, Mr. Howard. Don't look at it as a favor, but just a chance for all of us to become better acquainted," she said in a voice that only mothers have mastered.

Melvin Howard then surrendered to her wishes and sat down at the table. He opened his mouth as if to say something else but was quickly quieted by the overwhelming aroma of sizzling bacon and eggs. There was fresh brewed coffee on the stove and hot Danish in the oven. Together the smells mixed perfectly creating "Saturday". How could a man have a bad day with food that smelled that good in his stomach?

Melvin Howard was apparently thinking the same thoughts. I saw him sigh and try to disguise his hunger. Maybe it's the humbleness of it or the convenience, but I have never met a man who doesn't become elated by the scent of bacon and eggs in the morning.

Once brunch was served the four of us sat to eat. My mom didn't let us down either. The meal was terrific, and it made me feel proud to see Melvin Howard also enjoying his food. Every now and then my mother would look up from her plate to ask if everything was fine or if we wanted something more. She loved to cook for us, so on Saturday morning she was in her prime.

After the meal Melvin Howard thanked my mother for the food and her hospitality. Then my father spoke:

"Believe me Mr. Howard, we're happy to oblige." There was a pause.

"If you don't mind me asking," his pipe gripped tight between his teeth, "that old car of yours; I'll bet it needs a lot of maintenance. Wouldn't you rather get a new one?"

There was another pause. Melvin Howard shifted his weight in his chair, sipped some coffee, and smiled at my father.

" I don't mind you asking at all," said Melvin Howard.

In fact to me he seemed glad that my father had mentioned it.

"I guess a fair answer would be that old habits die hard," said Melvin Howard with a nostalgic look in his eye. . .

IV

It was summer time, school was out, the fish were biting, and the Indians were even off to a good start. All of these things combined for paradise to sixteen-year-old Melvin Howard, but this summer was even more special. He was sixteen, and the way he saw it sixteen was a landmark in his life for just last week he had gotten his driver's license. Now, he had proof that he was somebody and by the achievement of this success Melvin knew that he was destined for greatness.

Unfortunately, yet realistically, Melvin Howard was typical of most boys his age. He had a driver's license, but his parents still controlled the reins to his freedom because he did not have his own car. Even though he was able to use his father's car from time to time to help his mother run errands, he still spent countless hours driving his very own car in his imagination. Sometimes he drove an MGB convertible, roaring through the countryside, blurring by all the farmers on their tractors. Once in a while he would imagine that he took Elizabeth O'Donnell for short rides on Sunday afternoons. Both of them speeding off into the distance, enjoying the wind rippling through their hair, but mostly enjoying their freedom. "Freedom" and "new car", the words meant absolutely the same thing to Melvin. There was a tug on his line, but he ignored it. Instead he dropped back onto one elbow to relax and to really give his imagination a chance to go crazy. While his fingers swirled a dandelion until the golden flower popped from the stem, he allowed his dreaming eyes to wander across the Blanchard River. There was a road there, and even though it was not a much traveled route, cars did drive by at regular intervals. By closely watching each car that cruised, glided, zipped, or even sputtered down the road, he could feel his dreams of one day owning his own car. Most of the people in this area owned beat-up Fords or De Sotos with unimaginative coloring and noisy mufflers. These cars were fine for the timid or for the family who was trying to set a good example; however, these cars did not "ride like the wind," as Melvin often classified them. No, he needed something that showed no end to the freedom that he felt surging through his veins.

But, then, in the distance, he heard a new sound. It was definitely an engine, but it roared like a well-fed beast. It was moving very fast, spitting dust off the road into a giant cloud that chased after the car, never catching up. Melvin's ears perked like a squirrel's during hunting season, and he glued his eyes to the road to catch a glimpse of the speedster churning up the dust and humming like an electric generator. In just seconds, a sleek, shimmering white convertible sped by. Melvin didn't have much time to get a detailed description of the car, but he could tell by the shine of the paint and the speed it had to be special. The car captured his curiosity, mostly because of the vague impression it left for his imagination. He needed to know more, or even to just see it again.

Feeling unsatisfied yet inspired, Melvin tried half-heartedly to direct his attention back to fishing. He had already caught five crappie, a carp (which he threw back) and a small bullhead that was as ugly as the day was long. Methodically, he re-baited his hook, re-adjusted the sinker and bobber, and once again let the line cast out into the river. He would try to catch at least two more fish, and then he would head home, so he could recline underneath the big shady oak in their side yard and put a complete effort in on the mystery car that had just aroused his interest.

The fishing had been good for Melvin Howard all afternoon, so it wasn't long before the line gave a sharp tug and then another quick jerk that started to drag the bobber away from shore. Quickly, Melvin snapped the pole upward. There was a great deal of resistance on the pole. This was obviously a very big fish; but Melvin stayed with it. With his forearms tensed and his knuckles whitened he heaved and dragged the line closer to in. The water directly in front of him was broken by reckless and desperate splashes. Soon the fish would tire, and to speed up this process of fatigue, Melvin gave the pole another quick yank. This last pull yielded a flopping, struggling fish. It was a big fish, a pickerel; not the biggest he had ever seen, but nevertheless, a reasonably sized fish. Melvin knew that when his father saw this pickerel he would be very, proud for this was the first time Melvin had ever caught one.

With renewed vigor, the car forgotten, Melvin re-baited his conquering hook and cast his line back out in the murky river. If there was one pickerel, there had to be more. Intently, more like a hunter than a fisherman, Melvin watched his line and bobber float unimpeded further into the river. It floated easily until suddenly the line gave a short tug. It floated some more and then tugged again lightly. Melvin gripped the pole with both hands to ready himself. He knew from the initial tugs that this fish was not a pickerel, nor was it probably very big; however, Melvin Howard saw this as a new challenge and he set forth to conquer it, guppy or whale.

Just like before, he yanked the pole up quickly, but much to the boy's surprise the resistance on the line was even greater than it had been when the pickerel had first bitten. He tugged the pole up quickly again and still whatever was on the other end of the line refused to budge. Melvin gritted his teeth and tugged again, this time so hard that he fell backwards. When he fell, the resistance on the end of the line ceased much like finally getting a very tight lid off of a jar, and now the line floated back in on its own. Melvin sighed somewhat embarrassedly because it suddenly became obvious to him that the hook had really gotten snagged and when he fell backward the line had broken. So, disgustedly, Melvin pulled the line in to re-bait and to try again, however, when he raised the hook from the river it was not empty; but instead, he had hooked a rectangular piece of soaked leather - a wallet!

Hurriedly, Melvin unhooked the wallet and opened it. In the front flap there was a picture of a man in his late fifties, receding hairline, and a bushy moustache. It was a good picture unlike many drivers' licenses, thought Melvin, while he paged curiously through some other soaked photographs that were probably the man's family. Then Melvin opened the back flap, there was money. He pulled it out and started counting, his eyes growing wider as the sum of the money grew and grew.

"Two hundred eighty, three hundred, three hundred twenty...," whispered Melvin excitedly. There was definitely more money in that wallet than he had ever seen before, and he wasn't even done counting yet.

Finally, Melvin had counted the last bill, it was a five dollar bill and the smallest piece of currency in the wallet. Together, the bills totalled eight hundred and five dollars! Melvin's logic and emotions juggled each other as a confused, but excited grin, came across his face. What should he do, if anything at all?

Quickly he picked up his fishing pole and tackle and ran all the way home clutching the wallet in his free hand. Once home, he abruptly dropped his fishing gear on the front porch, and he bolted into the house and yelled, "Mom!" He was suddenly aware of his heavy breathing. It had been a long run home.

"Mom, guess what?" shouted the excited boy again. She was probably in the basement canning peaches.

Melvin clomped down the stairs and startled his mother half out of her wits.

"Sorry, mom. Guess what?" apologized Melvin, who was now managing to control his enthusiasm.

"What?" she said with one hand to her breast, stifling a scream when she realized that the intruder was her own son.

"I was fishing at the river, and boy, what a day!:

"That's nice dear. So, the fish were biting?"

"Yes, they were," said Melvin matter-of-factly, "but the best part was when the line got snagged."

She looked at him closely.

"I snagged a wallet with eight hundred and five dollars in it. I counted it," huffed Melvin in one last excited breath. Before his mother could speak Melvin held out the wallet and opened it to reveal the soaking wet green treasure.

Speechless, his mother took the money from the wallet and looked closely at the giant stack of cash in her hands. Secretly, she fought the urge to count it because never before had she touched so much money at once. "What should we do with it, Mom?" Her eyes were vacant, lost in the money before her. It is truly amazing how money has the unusual ability to turn whoever holds it into a dreamer. "Mom?" asked Melvin again softly touching her arm, which sufficiently dragged her from her trance. The right thing had to be done, but only if there was a "right thing". "Yes," she had gotten her voice back. "Landsakes, that is a lot of money!" she finished still exasperated.

Melvin nodded in agreement quietly wondering if she would be able to calm herself long enough to properly advise him on what should be done with the money. "Well honey," she began again, "we should find out whom the wallet belongs to."

Melvin agreed once again, however, this time he was reluctant since it had just occurred to him that his discovery would have to be returned to its more rightful owner.

He flipped back to the license at the front of the wallet. He read the name aloud to his mother, "Harold D. Owens, 1152 Jerome Road, Waterville, Ohio."

"My goodness, that's all the way over in the next county. I do wonder what he was doing along the river?" asked his mother.

This question was typical of his mother thought Melvin. He knew that it didn't really matter what the guy was doing down here because the only thing that mattered was that he had been and while here he had lost his wallet.

"Probably doing a little fishing," remarked Melvin.

She accepted his answer as logical.

"Let's just wait until your father gets home to see what he thinks. Waterville isn't very close you know."

"That's probably the best idea, Mom," and he kissed her appreciatively on the cheek.

With nothing else to be done about the money until his father returned from work Melvin went back to the front porch to begin cleaning the fish he had caught. He hated to clean fish, but he knew that his mother hated it even more. Besides, she was already busy canning the peaches, and both of them were very busy pondering the outcome of the cash.

That night after a wonderful dinner of pork chops and cooked apples, Melvin brought the wallet to his father. His father was a hard working man who seldom had a chance to relax. One of these rare relaxing moments came for Melvin Howard's father each night after dinner when he read the newspaper in his over-stuffed arm chair while he smoked a pipe with a crisp, yet mellow tobacco. When his father's attentions were directed toward the newspaper it was often hard to get him to fully listen to anything more.

Melvin thought about waiting until his father had at least finished the sports page, his favorite section; but he knew he couldn't wait any longer. After all, finding eight hundred and five dollars was important enough to interrupt his father's relaxation, and if the money didn't seem worth it, the monstrous pickerel Melvin had caught that afternoon would be a good reason for the interruption.

"Dad," Melvin decide immediately to forget the pickerel and go straight to the money.

"Yes son, what is it?" The words his father spoke were tight because he spoke with the pipe clenched tight between his teeth. This was a characteristic that Melvin felt made pipe smokers far more impressive than any other smoker.

"While I was fishing today," he paused long enough to notice his mother walk into the room. She had been listening from the kitchen while she finished washing the dishes.

Melvin then spoke again, "When I was fishing I snagged a wallet"

"Oh yeah?" His father's attention was still not entirely devoted to anything but the article he was reading about the Indians' current streak.

"There was some money in it. A lot of money," continued Melvin.

Slowly the newspaper began to lower. "What? How much?" his father was finally interested.

Eight hundred and five," said Melvin without expression while he waited momentarily for his father's reaction.

"Where is it?" asked his father.

Melvin handed the now-dry wallet to his father who immediately opened it and removed the stack of bills.

"Good golly Moses," remarked Melvin's father, trying to maintain his calm, cool, collected fatherly image.

"How did you find this, son?" he asked, eyes blazing with wonder.

Melvin then told his story again about how he had discovered the money during his afternoon of fishing. His father listened closely so he would not miss a single detail of the discovery.

"My goodness." His father was still shocked. He counted the money himself to re-affirm the total of eight hundred and five dollars. Then he flipped to the driver's license of Harold D. Owens at the front of the wallet.

"Well," Melvin's father had arrive at a solution, "the way I see it we've got to return it somehow." Honesty was something Melvin's father had prided himself on, and therefore, this was the best solution and the only one that would please his father.

"We can take it to the local police and have them keep it until Mr. Owens claims it himself; and if he doesn't claim it within sixty days you get to keep all of the money, Melvin." This idea sounded good but sixty days was a long time to wait for the money, and yet, there wasn't even a guarantee that the money would go to him anyway.

"Or, our second choice is," his father continued, "we can drive up to Waterville and deliver this money to Mr. Owens personally. There might be a reward."

The choice was Melvin's because the money was his discovery. His father had shown him his options, but there was absolutely no way his father would decide this dilemma for him. Another philosophy that Melvin's father firmly believed in was that a man should make his own decisions and then live with the consequences, good or bad. This was tough because Melvin could see good sides and bad sides to both of his options. What was worse was that he knew his father knew which of the two options was best. It was helpful to himself as well as to Mr. Owens, since the money was actually his. By bringing the police in it would create a greater inconvenience for Mr. Owens as well as for himself because he would be stuck waiting around for a number of days, not knowing whether he was to receive a reward or not. On the other hand, by bringing the money to Mr. Owens himself, Melvin would at least gain the satisfaction that the man got his money back.

"Let's deliver the money ourselves," said Melvin definitively. His father smiled to indicate to Melvin that he had made the right decision.

The next day Melvin and his father left after breakfast for Waterville in his father's black De Soto. It was a perfect day for a drive, sunny and warm with a comfortable breeze. The drive to Waterville would take about forty-five minutes to an hour since they had to drive on back township routes to a place that Melvin's father had only been to twice before. The best way to go was to follow the bridge that allowed them into Waterville. Once they crossed the old iron bridge, Melvin liked what he saw. Waterville was small, but it was bigger than the small town in which Melvin had lived all his life.

To get to Jerome Road, where Harold D. Owens lived wasn't hard at all. Mr. Owens' home was a lavish farmhouse that stretched out over what seemed like miles of land. The farm reminded Melvin of the Southern plantations that he had learned about in his history lessons in school. The driveway to the Owens' house was long and winding and made of gravel. At the end of the drive was a cul-de-sac and a horse stable. Beyond the stable was a small, abrupt hill that tumbled into a tiny brook. The whole farm looked like something Melvin had seen before either in a magazine or on a Christmas card.

After ringing the bell, that sounded like that of a cathedral, Melvin and his father waited a long time on the porch. Finally, just when they were ready to resign themselves to the fact that Mr. Owens was not home, the door latch thudded and the huge door was pulled open. In the doorway was a smartly dressed man wearing an ascot and a confused look probably because he did not recognize the people standing on the porch.

"Yes, what do you want?" sternly asked the man in the doorway.

"We need to speak with Harold D. Owens," said Melvin's father. "Does he live here?" This question was necessary since the man in the doorway did not resemble the picture on Mr. Owens' driver's license.

"Yes, he lives here," said the man arrogantly, "but he is just preparing to have his lunch on the back patio."

"With all due respect, sir," said Melvin's father. He was using words to speak to this man that Melvin had never heard him use before.

"We do not wish to bother Mr. Owens, but I think what we have for him will make him quite happy," said Melvin's father.

"Oh indeed, what are you selling that Mr. Owens could possibly want?" asked the man in the doorway showing his annoyance with Melvin and his father.

"No sir, we are not salesmen," said Melvin's father, now showing offense to this doorman's undue stuffiness. "We, or my son, I mean, has found Mr. Owens' money and wallet."

This time the doorman's face took on a look of surprise, and then, Melvin held the wallet out for the man to see and study with his own eyes. Immediately, he showed them through the house to the back patio. On their way through the house it was hard not to notice the elegant interior features that wonderfully complemented the royal exterior. There were gilded, crystalline chandeliers, ceiling fans, spacious carpeted rooms, a spiral staircase that seemed to lead directly to heaven, and most memorable of all, the giant stuffed heads of the big game animals that lined the halls. It was truly an amazing place.

The back patio, which more closely resembled what Melvin had imagined the Hanging Gardens of Babylon to look like, had wrought iron stools with padded cushions and a beautiful little table with a glass top. There was also a built-in swimming pool, the first that Melvin had ever seen, fenced in by tall, leafy hedges that were shaped more squarely and perfectly than blocks of marble. At the small patio table sat a small, hunched man in his late fifties. He had a receding hairline and a bushy moustache. It was safe to assume, thought Melvin, that this man was Harold D. Owens. Although he looked distinguished, even old for his age, thought Melvin, he definitely didn't look rich.

"Hello, gentlemen, how are you?" Mr. Owens had spoken to them before the doorman had introduced them.

"Fine, thank you," responded Melvin's father.

"That's good. What can I help you with?" smiled Mr. Owens. He seemed to be a good-natured man, and he had a Southern accent that added even more credibility to his good nature.

"You are Mr. Harold D. Owens?" asked Melvin's father. Mr. Owens assured them that he was "the one and only".

"Mr. Owens, my son here has found your wallet and some money we think belongs to you," said Melvin's father handing the wallet over. Mr. Owens quickly grabbed the wallet like a beggar who might grab a morsel of bread crust from a generous hand. He immediately emptied the wallet of all its cash and counted it. His facial expression was a corporation of surprise and joy and then satisfaction when he apparently realized that all the money was intact.

"How did you find this?" he asked gleaming like a child on Christmas morning.

"While I was fishing I snagged it," said Melvin finally seeing this as an appropriate time to speak. After all, he had found the wallet and he was sixteen-years-old; so he should not let his father speak entirely for him.

"This wallet has been missing for over a month," gasped the rich gentleman. "I should never have been carrying this much cash with me, but old habits die hard," he said. . .

Melvin Howard just sat there then reminiscing about the beautiful house in Waterville and Harold D. Owens silently while we all looked at him closely. We were on the edge of our seats, impatiently awaiting the end of Melvin Howard's story and the undoubted point to which he was arriving. Yet, he didn't speak. He sipped his coffee and sighed a laugh as he came back to the table from his memories.

"So, did he give you a reward?" interjected my mother asking the question we all wanted to know the answer to.

"In a way, he did," said Melvin Howard vaguely. He kept smiling and then he went on, "You see, that day my father and I stayed for lunch with Mr. Owens. In fact, we visited with him all afternoon. He was very impressive, and he was impressed with us nearly as much as we were with him," added Melvin Howard modestly.

"Like my father, Mr. Owens also felt honesty was a great personal philosophy to follow," he paused momentarily to take another sip of his coffee. "He said that he had made his money by being honest, and he felt due to my honesty I would also be successful some day."

"So that day Mr. Owens offered me a job working on his farm. He said it would be hard work, but that I would be paid and well-taken care of. To do this I would have to live on the farm away from my parents, which made my father uneasy at first; however, Mr. Owens said he didn't believe in working on weekends, so I could go home after work every Friday if I wished. Plus, it would only be for the summer months."

"As it turned out, I was given my mother and father's blessing to take the job. I loved it. I usually worked outside doing whatever was needed, and I was paid ten dollars a day, which was very good wages for a boy my age then. In fact, I worked out so well Mr. Owens kept me on every summer until I got out of college."

"I owe a lot to that man. He set me up with my first bank account. I fell in love for the first time during my third summer on that farm with a girl from another farm further up the road a-piece. Mr. Owens even helped me go to college. One helluva man."

"Mr. Howard?" this time it was my father interrupting Melvin Howard's reflective moment, "I'm not sure I understand. How does your story about

Mr. Owens' farm relate to your old car?"

"Oh," it seemed like Melvin Howard was thoroughly analyzing my father's question as if he himself didn't' have an answer for it.

"You see, because of that job, I was able to afford my first car," said Melvin Howard his smile growing wider, "and that car in front of your house right now is that same car!"

The car was more than a car to Melvin Howard, for it stood for hard work, opportunity, and above all else, independence and honesty - all of these things combined had made Harold D. Owens successful as well as Melvin Howard's mentor. Trading in the old car for a new one might be like trading a portion of his own life, and the thought of driving a new car for just a means of more reliable transportation seemed trivial and dull. The old car possessed character, and furthermore, that character was a direct reflection of its owner, Melvin Howard.

V

One week after Melvin Howard spent Saturday brunch with us my father and I saw him uptown while we were running some errands. It was strange, I thought, now that we've met this man we see him on a regular basis. I wondered how many times we had actually seen him before we had met him. On this particular day uptown our path crossed with Melvin Howard's at the drugstore. We were picking up some vitamins for my mother when Melvin Howard stepped in behind us.

"Hello, my friends. How are you today?" His voice was introduction enough for us to accurately identify him because he always spoke in the same friendly tone that echoed of nostalgia, worldliness, and knowledge, yet it soothed warmly and simplistically like the fire he had built in the hearth that cold, rainy afternoon when he and I had first met.

"Hi!" I smiled back at him.

"Hello, Mr. Howard," returned my father shaking hands with Melvin Howard.

"What's new?" he asked.

"Not a lot. We're just picking up some vitamins for my mom," I replied.

"That's good. Me, I'm having some sinus trouble lately. It's been so darn damp outside these past couple weeks," said Melvin Howard squeezing the bridge of his nose between two fingers to further indicate that he was having sinus troubles.

"So, I'm picking up this prescription from my doctor. Says it will take away some of the pressure," he continued as he held out a small slip of paper so we could see the prescription. I couldn't read it, but it was evident that there was some type of language written on it, or scrawled would be a better description. I looked briefly at the prescription then back at Melvin Howard's face. He didn't look sick.

"You don't look sick," I said thinking aloud. Just then my father gave me a sharp nudge in my back, which I'm sure Melvin Howard failed to see because parents are good at finding and using forms of corporal punishment that can be used in public without having the public think that they are child abusers. Once again, my imagination was running rampant.

Melvin Howard chuckled, recognizing the innocence of my question more than the complete disregard for tact.

"Well, I'm not really sick just a little uncomfortable. To be honest I don't want to even get these pills because it seems like such a waste of money. After the pills are gone I'll still have sinus troubles. Sinus troubles are as incurable as cancer, except they won't kill me. So, since I'm not a doctor, I'll take his advice and keep on taking the pills to be comfortable until this damp weather breaks," said Melvin Howard calmly. After Melvin Howard had gotten his prescription he walked with us outside to our car. My dad and I were both poised to say our "good-byes" when Melvin Howard spoke to me.

"Martin, remember when I told you about working for Harold D. Owens over in Waterville?"

I nodded.

"Well, I was wondering if you might be interested in helping me out after school with some of the work I've got to do around my house?" He looked closely, first at me, then at my father.

I looked up at my father for the right answer.

"Mr. Howard, what would you want Martin to do? He doesn't have much experience," asked my father curiously.

"Well, he won't be doing much at first. But, I will work with him to help him along. Mostly, he will help me get my work done faster and more efficiently than I could do alone," said Melvin Howard smiling at me.

"What do you say, Martin?" asked my father. "It sounds like good experience."

"While you're in school we'll just work on the weekends, but if you work out okay, this summer we'll up your hours," said Melvin Howard. My father was apparently convinced, but I wasn't sure if I was convinced. This was very sudden, and I was confused because I wasn't sure if I was ready for the responsibility that it might involve. Yet, Melvin Howard was so kind, it was hard to say "no" to him, especially when in reality it was me who he was doing the favor for.

"Oh yes, and you'll be paid," Melvin Howard continued. He was now speaking words that I had never heard before, except when my father and mother offered to pay me a couple dollars for cleaning the house while they were gone one afternoon.

"Really?" I asked still amazed.

"Of course. You can't work well without any incentive!" proclaimed Melvin Howard proudly.

"How much will you be able to pay?" asked my father not very discretely.

"I'll start paying him ten dollars a day until the first of the new year. If he works out fine by that time I'll pay him twenty dollars a day with chances for future raises."

That was good money, especially for a boy my age, considering he had never even seen me work before.

"You can start this Saturday," continued Melvin Howard.

VI

So I agreed to help Melvin Howard starting Saturday. According to him we were going to clean out the basement; which oddly enough I was looking forward to because I was trying to imagine what Melvin Howard's basement was like. Judging from the stories of his experiences, I was sure that his basement would be riddled with mementos and other nostalgia that was sure to capture the curiosity of a highly imaginative seventh grader like me. On Saturday then, I went to Melvin Howard's house on my reborn bicycle. It was about ten o'clock; which had forced our traditional Saturday morning brunch to be earlier. My mother was not entirely happy about the time in which I was to begin work, but she never really verbalized her discontent on the matter. I could tell though. It showed in her cooking efforts that morning. Everything had seemed rushed and trivial, as if the tradition was gone and the mere necessity of nourishment was the only thing considered. The food was good as usual, however, even at that young age I was somewhat of a traditionalist and with my usual Saturday morning ritual abruptly altered my egg-filled stomach still unfortunately felt numb and empty.

I rang the doorbell at Melvin Howard's house. It sounded like an off-key trumpet, definitely unusual, and definitely obnoxious, I thought. The large inside door creaked open to reveal the smiling face of my employer.

"Good morning, Martin!" he exclaimed enthusiastically.

"Good morning, sir, " said I fighting the sudden urge to yawn.

"C'mon in boy. I've got to get dressed for our work. Do you want a glass of grapefruit juice?" he asked hospitably.

He showed me into the kitchen, which now smelled of burned bacon. He offered me a chair at the table, poured me a large glass of grapefruit juice from the refrigerator, and handed me the morning newspaper.

"I'll be just a couple minutes," he said. He was eager to start work, while the only thing I was eager to do was to somehow get rid of the grapefruit juice without actually drinking it, nor having Melvin Howard perceive me as ungracious for his kindness. After all, he didn't have to offer me anything to drink since I had just finished my own breakfast.

"All the sections of the paper are still there, so pick what you like," he said bustling off down a hallway that extended from the kitchen.

"Thanks," I mumbled staring confusedly at the glass of juice before me. It was so cloudy. I couldn't see how any liquid of that consistency or that color could be good. The glass was very cold, which in itself might be refreshing on a hot humid day. Yet, I was leery. Grapefruit juice was bitter, a taste that could never be refreshing.

"By the way, read 'Doonesbury' today. It's very funny," Melvin Howard's voice boomed down the hallway. "I certainly got a charge out of it," he continued with a forced laugh.

As if I were commanded to read "Doonesbury", I paged through the paper until I came to the comics. I read the comic and chuckled slightly and absent mindedly, for I didn't fully understand the satire. In fact, I had never really understood the "Doonesbury" comic strip because the political satire always went over my head. It was weird, but it seemed like the reader had to be tuned into current events just to laugh at a comic anymore. That was the trend anyway. It seemed like everyone wanted Richard Nixon and Watergate to be the butt of their jokes. Unfortunately, for me and the cartoonist, in this case, I rarely read the paper so I was not well-professed in current events. I was not pigheaded about reading the news; I would just have rather read my fictional stories because it was far better to imagine what might be happening than to worry about what was really happening.

Melvin Howard came back down the hallway whistling "Route 66" and buttoning up an old flannel shirt. Nervously, I took a sip of my grapefruit juice. It was bitter and I winced noticeably. Melvin Howard chuckled, "Don't really like that stuff do you?"

"No, no. I like it." I lied, but even still I prepared for my next bitter sip.

"No, you really don't. I can tell," answered Melvin Howard.

Instead of answering him, I blushed and took another sip and swallowed it wincing.

"That's okay," he started again, and he patted my shoulder. "You'll get used to it so well that you'll love it."

"I don't know about that." I had now managed an embarrassed smile.

"Grapefruit is something you have to acquire a taste for, but after you do you'll be glad you did."

"Why?" I asked.

"Well, for one, it's real good for you. Lots of vitamins, even more than orange juice," said Melvin Howard as he poured himself a tall glass of the juice. I watched him take a long drink.

"Aah," said Melvin Howard wiping some stray droplets off his moustache.

"I used to feel the same way about grapefruit as you do now," he went on holding the glass before him as if he were studying it. "But my grandfather introduced me to it because he convinced me that you should give everything a chance since looks can be deceiving." He looked at me intently and smiled.

33

"You see," he went on, "you can't see everything that's good in grapefruit juice right off, but the good stuff - nutrients, vitamins, and such are definitely all there. Yes, indeed, you have got to give everything a chance."

He had that familiar far-off look in his eyes again, so I listened closely.

"Martin, someday, you may have to go to a place where you will have to eat foods that you have never seen or tasted before, and some of it may not even seem like it should be food to you; but by disciplining your taste buds you can acquire the taste for anything."

"Look at potatoes," he continued. "Potatoes grow underground and they're roots, technically; yet the potato is one of the most important sources of starch and carbohydrates known to the human diet. Also, they're easy to fix, and they taste good just about any way you fix them."

"But, Martin, it's good to be skeptical about things, and it's impossible to like everything. . ."

VII

Melvin Howard was just three months beyond his twenty-second birthday when he graduated from college, and since he had finished in the middle of the year, he had plenty of time to search for a job. Even though he had the proper credentials to get a job that he liked, he was more interested in doing something exciting to unwind from four years of nerve-racking college coursework. All his life he had wanted to travel, especially since he had spent his summers working on Mr. Owens' farm. Harold D. Owens literally lived a life of adventure and Melvin wanted a similar opportunity. Now, that he was out of school he had the chance, and his time belonged to him for the time being. He had saved some money from working at Mr. Owens' farm, so expenses were not that important. Besides, if one truly wanted to have an adventure it might be necessary to pick up odd jobs along the way to help finance one's lust for adventure. Harold D. Owens had done it this way, therefore, so would Melvin Howard.

The only drawback he was having was that he really did not want to go alone. Off the top of his head, he could only think of one friend that might be willing to take some time out to join him in his excursion. The man's name was Paul Cassini. He was an Italian kid from Brooklyn whom Melvin had met at college. Paul came to Ohio Northern on a partial academic and athletic scholarship to play football. Paul's position was defensive back, and while he was not a starter he had achieved all-state honors in high school in New York for both football and track. Paul and Melvin became friends when they lived next door to one another in the dormitory during their sophomore year. Both young men held similar interests, socially and intellectually, so they developed a good friendship. Melvin knew that Paul was the perfect candidate to take with him. Plus, Paul could be relied upon better than his other friends because he was loyal and held the same zest for adventure as Melvin.

Hesitating no longer, Melvin dialed the number Paul had given him just after the end of their graduation ceremony. Paul would be in Brooklyn with his parents until he found the right job.

The phone rang twice, and then once more before it was answered.

"Yello." The voice that answered was deeply ethnic and soft and definitely feminine. It was Paul's mother, whom Melvin had met once when she and Paul's father came to Ohio to see him as part of their vacation one year.

"Hello, Mrs. Cassini, this is Melvin Howard, a friend of Paul's from college."

"Yes?"

"Is he at home? I need to ask him a question," he suddenly hoped that he had not sounded blunt.

"Jus' one moment please," she said. Her voice was slow and deliberate, testing each word carefully like an ice skater trying to avoid the thin spots on a frozen lake.

He did not have to wait long before he heard her call to Paul in Italian. Melvin then heard Paul's rough-cut, Brooklyn accented voice yell back to his mother's call.

"Awright Ma', I'm comin'!"

There was a short pause.

"Hi. What's up?" Paul said quickly. That was one quality that Melvin had never liked about Paul. He always seemed to use an impatient tone of voice that made him sound like he was keeping the world's busiest schedule and that it was incredibly inconvenient for him to talk to another person. He had originally taken some getting used to Melvin recalled.

"Pauli! How's it going for you?" said Melvin.

"Pretty good, I 'spose," Paul snickered cockily, which Melvin readily accepted as Paul's way of showing that he was glad Melvin had called after all.

"I've got a great opportunity for you," Melvin started in. Trying very hard not to forget any of the details of his idea for the long-sought after adventure, Melvin explained the trip to Paul. And as originally guessed, Paul loved the idea. He agreed, and he would go with Melvin. Their adventure was to be a photo safari/exploration in the Congo, a place Melvin and Paul had dreamed of seeing ever since they had read Conrad's Heart of Darkness for their British literature course.

The plans were set. Melvin would meet Paul in New York where they would catch a ship to Africa. The trip would be long, but for now, the thought of the adventure itself surged vibrantly in Melvin's veins. Melvin wanted to feel the same blistering heat that Marlowe felt in Conrad's novel. He wanted to see all of the marvels that the jungle could offer. He wanted to engage in the same rough-and-tumble lifestyle associated with the harnassing of a relatively new frontier. So, at the end of the month, Melvin left for New York City by train and several days later he and his college friend Paul were crossing the Atlantic Ocean.

Paul was as equally excited about the journey as Melvin. They both constantly talked about what they would hope to see when they actually arrived in the Congo. Both men were also admittedly nervous because soon they would find themselves in a land that in their minds seemed to be the furthest extreme of the earth, a concept their imaginations never tired of trying to picture now that it was so close.

At the end of five days, the ship finally docked. Here was the destination - Africa. It was early morning, yet the land all around seemed to sweat from the heat. Nevertheless, Melvin and Paul welcomed the perspiration. They had even longed for it; and now, it was here for them. They experienced this sensational blast of heat, and everywhere, the land smelled moist, warm and thick with lush vegetation. Melvin sensed something else hidden by the early morning blanket of fog that surrounded the ship. Everything he felt and sensed was wild and unchanged by complete civilization. The adventure had begun, for Africa was really here. It was alive, and it called out its welcome to Melvin and Paul as paradise might call to any man. The sounds of the wild were out there as well. The tiny bungalow where they stayed was overtaken by the sounds of wild birds shrieking and cawing in the dark forest. The sun was sweltering; but despite the intolerable heat, both Melvin and Paul were impatient. They wanted to do everything and see everything, but they could not truly begin their adventure until the next day when they would meet their guide. Being strangers to this land, Paul and Melvin decided that it was best not to take undue risks like the kind that might get them lost in the rain forest.

The evening moved into night, but not like any nightfall the young men had ever seen before. The sky was black like a vampire's cape, and the air captivated both the extreme pleasure of serenity and the extreme discomfort of the unknown; for even though all of the Congo had been discovered and charted for years, Melvin and Paul were new to this world, and they felt mystified by its uniqueness and solemnity. They also, however, felt like intruders in a land that would be far better off if man were to never see it, much less touch it. Melvin was sure in his mind that Conrad's character, Marlowe in Heart of Darkness had a similar feeling when he first came face-to-face with this innocently primitive world.

There were sounds in the night just as there were in the daytime, but these were different, for these sounds seemed to grasp the imagination and attach themselves to the shapes and faces of creatures, terrible, carnivorous animals that man had yet to discover and understand. The Congo, Melvin decided, definitely belonged entirely to God and Nature, a message made so heavily apparent that it was hard to imagine man serving a realistic place in this realm of lush, steamy jungles, sooty nights, blazing heat, and misunderstood creations, both man and beast alike.

Eventually both men fell into a restless sleep, the type of sleep that is present during the humid summer months. However, this type of sleep that is often broken by tossing and turning when men are wrestling with their dreams proved to be, nevertheless, satisfactory to Melvin and Paul; for neither of them desired rest. They desired to be awake and for the soft, yet sinister black night to retreat far over the western horizon, allowing the brilliant, searing African sun to take command again.

As always, the never-ending night did subside into morning. The dawn broke in the Congo with a rush as the vibrantly colored macaws screamed outside the bungalow at a maddening din. Melvin and Paul both jolted violently in their cots, scared momentarily and suddenly wide awake. Paul swung his legs over the side of the cot to face Melvin.

"Beats the hell out of our roosters," said Paul scratching the back of his head.

Melvin laughed. Paul was quick-witted and exhaustively funny when properly inspired. Melvin too hopped up from his cot and then walked across the matted floor to a wash basin that sat on a small, cheaply constructed bureau table across the room, the only one in the bungalow. Quickly he splashed his face several times with the cold water in the bowl. Magically, the cool water transformed him into the person he recognized everyday to be himself. It was envigorating. He took a brief moment to notice his appearance in the mirror and decided that shaving was utterly out of the question. A little stubble on a man's cheeks and chin added to his character. After all, primitive man did not shave his whiskers so it seemed only appropriate that he should avoid shaving while on this adventure.

Once they were dressed in safari attire they waited outside in front of their bungalow for the guide that they had arranged for. The guide when he arrived, was not entirely unlike what they expected, except for the landrover that he pulled up in. It was a rickety vehicle, but highly appropriate for the grasslands of Africa. The guide himself was a small, frail man with skin the tone of mahogany. He spoke slowly and uncomfortably. But, remarkably, he spoke English. Melvin and Paul learned that the guide's name was 'Tubu' and that he would be with them every step of the way; plus he had promised to show them some of his favorite sights in his homeland, ones not on the schedule that had been originally arranged. This extra courtesy of the guide gave Paul and Melvin a certain sense of flattery that fueled their eagerness to get started on the first day's adventures.

The landrover grunted when the guide shifted it into first gear.

"She is a little grouchy today," he said apologetically as the landrover lurched forward jerkily.

Melvin forced himself to laugh, but he was uneasy suddenly for it seemed the landrover wasn't in good shape and the possibility of a breakdown in the middle of the jungle was frightening.

The landrover did struggle, but it managed, bouncing recklessly over the hills and dirt paths like a super ball just slammed off of the asphalt in a school yard. Soon Melvin forgot the uncomfortable ride and the motion sickness the ride was giving him because he started to notice the life around him. The plant life was by far the most noticeable because it was everywhere. Everything was so very green, and the trees echoed with the sounds of other life forms. Noisy tropical birds were abundant, and the one Melvin found himself most intrigued by was what the guide referred to as the greater horned bill. It was a black bird, not much unlike a crow, with a huge golden bill. The bill itself seemed to be divided into two parts. The guide had informed Melvin and Paul that the bird used the top part of the bill, the horn, to dig through the bark of trees, which made finding grubs and insects to eat much easier. This was the first creature they photographed.

The landrover continued even though the brush was starting to get very thick. Finally, the inevitable happened. Tubu stopped the landrover abruptly, which caused the disagreeable machine to backfire black, oily soot out its tailpipe.

"We can not drive any further, sirs," Tubu said politely.

"Why not?" asked Paul. The bluntness of Paul's question made Melvin embarrassed for him.

The guide was luckily not taken aback by Paul's abrasive question. After all, they needed to treat him with utmost kindness since their survival virtually rested in his hands.

Tubu hopped out of the landrover and simply said, "Too much trees." The answer was obvious as to why the landrover could not continue. The forest ahead of them was lush with greenness and the trees were so high they nearly blocked out the noon-day sun. Steam seemed to rise from the ground for the humidity was nearly one hundred percent and immediately this started a flood of sweat dripping from each man's brow and armpits. The damp, hot leaves all around them cast off a heavy perfumed scent that foliage often does after a thundershower. The scent was overbearing yet primitively pleasing. The jungle they were stepping into held an eeriness about it that Melvin had never before experienced. The sensation tingled up and down his spine in the form of excitement. Fear was there too, but it was more subconscious than apparent. The gripping part of this new sensation, however, was loneliness. Suddenly the forest seemed too deep, too vast, and Melvin felt that his being there seemed utterly wrong and foolish. Still, it was curiosity that beckoned him to follow as Tubu headed into the dark green uncertainty, armed with only a walking shaft.

"The day had been long but wonderful in every sense of the imagination," thought Melvin as he lounged in a hot bath. The water was soothing and it felt good to be able to retreat to this one civilized, and familiar, luxury after spending the day behind the primitive mask of the jungle. Melvin Howard slowly rolled his head back, sighed, and decided that he was happy for what he had.

The day did provide both he and Paul with some good photos. While in the jungle they saw a strange antelope called an "okapi", which Tubu had told them was a rare sight because the animal is very shy and is usually only found deep in the rain forest. They also photographed several different monkeys, more parrots, a lemur, crocodiles from a distance, and a very small deer-like antelope called a "reebok." Paul was also fortunate to get a photograph of some large, neon-colored moths. The animals were like no others that Melvin had ever seen before. He was glad that he had taken the opportunity to see these things realizing that it was a shame for the people who never get the chance to see Africa; or even worse, for the people who might never want to see Africa.

After both Melvin and Paul had finished an extensive soak in the bathtub they decided to walk into the village. There was small bar there with a restaurant at which they could get something to eat since both of them were famished. The village was the equivalence of a block away and there seemed to always be a lot of activity there no matter what time it was, but this was understandable since there was no other place around the area that even hinted at civilization.

Once in town, it was easy to find the tavern for it was where everyone was. The place inside was smokey and loud. There were fortunately two chairs at the bar, and Paul motioned to them with a nod of his head. Melvin understood and together they fought their way through the sweaty, drunken crowd, occasionally side-stepping a misguided, ambling drunk or a waitress with a full load of drinks perched on a tray she cradled up high on one hand to keep it out of the reach of the many gesturing hands that might spill the drinks accidently.

Sitting at the bar, Paul took the liberty to order two beers, which were lukewarm and foamy, anything but thirst-quenching. It was all right though because the drinks were inexpensive. Because the dollar was worth so much more than the currency used in the village, their American money would go far. There were no menus at the bar, so Melvin stopped the bartender.

"We need some menus, sir."

"We ain't got minus," the bartender said pausing to spit chewing tobacco into a large paper cup. "What you want?"

He was a burly white man with a phenomenally large beer belly, and he spoke with an accent that probably placed him as being originally from the Southeastern United States.

"What do you have to eat here?" Melvin asked forcing down another sip of his beer. The foam still had not settled.

"Well, the only thing we got left is cobra," said the bartender without smiling. He was serious.

Melvin suddenly became aware of his appetite slipping away from him. Out of the corner of his eye he saw Paul surprisingly choke on his foamy beer.

"Does it taste like chicken?" Paul asked trying to maintain his wit.

"What ?" the bartender asked dumbfounded.

A millennium passed as the three men stood in silence, each one taking turns exchanging dumb looks with one of the others.

"Well, it ain't that dif'cult a deesishun to make, boys," said the bartender putting a toothpick between his teeth. He had disgust in his voice and cheap whiskey on his breath, and instantly Melvin wanted to gag.

"He's right Paul," Melvin began, "Are we going to eat or not?"

Paul looked thoughtful for a moment. The decision seemed to be entirely up to him.

"Well, we are in a place that we've never been to before." Paul was thinking out loud as he rubbed his chin with his thumb then he bit the nail nervously, yet discretely.

"Yeah, Paul, this place certainly isn't America," returned Melvin. Both men encouraged each other since people seldom find comfort in crossing new horizons alone.

"That's true too," Paul was still thinking.

"What do you say Paul?" Melvin was becoming aggressively instrumental in the final decision since blame can only apply to individuals. Still, the outcome would be easier if Paul made the decision on his own. "We should try something new since we are in a new place," he concluded.

Paul would go for it. It was not that Melvin was so anxious to try cobra, but he did not feel it was right to be judgmental. Africa was not the place he was used to, and silently he wondered if an African would feel squeamish about eating pizza or hamburgers or hot dogs. Yet, somehow the parallel wasn't the same. The issue was not whether an African was going to eat a hot dog, but whether he, Melvin Howard was going to eat cobra. The idea still made him cringe, and he fought a sudden urge to shiver with disgust.

By now the bartender was mixing a drink for a bearded African whom had just taken the stool next to Paul. From what Melvin could see the bearded man was drinking something similar to a gin and tonic except the bartender had added grenadine to make the drink a pale pink color. For some reason, the drink just did not fit the atmosphere of the bar. But, with a feeling of guilt for once again being judgmental, Melvin passed the thought from his mind.

"Hey sir," Paul said, speaking to the bearded African. "Sir, if you were to eat here, in this place, what would you recommend?" Paul said quietly and quite seriously.

The bearded man turned to face Paul. 'God, was his nose large,' thought Melvin nearly out loud, but again, he felt the guilt he had already felt twice in the evening. He was being judgmental of another new encounter, and he suddenly thought for a moment that he had spent too much time in rural Ohio and that his views on anything different from what he already knew might never change.

"Well, I am very sorry, sir," spoke the African. His accent was similar to a British accent. "I have never been to this tavern before myself for I am travelling from Johannesburg to a missionary my people have established here in the jungle. It is a long journey, so I am stopping to quench my thirst and rest for the night.

"Oh," remarked Paul blandly rolling his eyes.   ,

"Although," continued the bearded African, "if this place serves a plate of fried cobra, I would recommend that. It is very tasty and delicate, yet very rich in flavor if it is prepared well."

Paul and Melvin both looked at the man with disbelief and then at the bartender who was smiling dumbly and widely, listening to their conversation.

41

"Oh yes," the bearded African continued for he had seen the skeptical looks on their faces. "I particularly enjoy mine served with hot peppers." The man was serious and for some reason it seemed to Melvin that they had no choice now that Paul had acquired his second opinion.

"I'll take an order of 'food'," Melvin and Paul said simultaneously even though neither could actually say the word, "cobra".

"All right," drooled the toothpick chewing bartender. Melvin was certain that his grandmother had warned him about people like this bartender. No matter, their fate was sealed for in a few moments his meal of fried cobra would be there for him to eat. It was not hard now for Melvin to imagine himself not actually being in Africa, but instead he was some place even further away from home, perhaps Mars.

'Martians probably eat cobra,' thought Melvin restlessly.

Paul was not speaking. He was drinking. It seemed to Melvin as if Paul was fixed in a quest to get to the bottom of his glass for he was chugging the Scotch he had just ordered like water. The last drop of Scotch slid out of the glass and through Paul's lips as the ice cubes tumbled forward to follow the alcohol. Paul allowed one ice cube to enter his mouth, and he sucked on it for a moment then chewed it noisily.

"Bartender, set my friend and me up with another round. Scotch," proclaimed Paul. His voice had risen an octave. 'Effects of the alcohol,' decided Melvin.

"Oh, what the hell," Paul was getting feisty now. "Bartender, mix another drink for this man here too," said Paul patting the shoulder of the bearded African whose glass was now also dry.

"Thank you, sir. You are a generous man," commented the African.

Well, Paul wasn't generous, he was getting drunk. Melvin remembered a time in a downtown Cleveland bar after an Indians-Yankees game when Paul became too generous and could not pay the tab at the night's end. Luckily for both of them, Melvin had had enough money to cover them, but he was left broke for over a week until Paul could find a way to repay him.

"What are you doing?" Melvin said chuckling at his friend's growing drunkenness. "Why are you chugging those drinks? I don't have enough to cover you for the rest of our trip," said Melvin.

"Well, in a couple more minutes I'm going to be eating a snake, a poisonous snake," Paul paused effectively. Drunks were always such dramatic speakers.

"So?" Melvin encouraged.

"So, I'm trying to get drunk enough so that I'll eat damn near anything." Paul's logic was demented, but Melvin laughed any way.

"Hey, I've always heard that whiskey cures a snake bite," said Paul as he slurped another sip from his glass. This time Paul's little pun forced Melvin to snort a swig of his own drink up his nose.

After wiping his nose with a bar napkin Melvin replied chuckling, "True, but does snake bite cure alcohol poisoning?" Paul smiled, forced a laugh, and chomped another ice cube.

Melvin noticed that the African also seemed to be giggling slightly; however, it was hard to tell what exactly was causing his laughter. Maybe he was laughing with the two young Americans and their puns, but yet, Melvin was paranoid that the African was really laughing at their culture shock. To the African, eating cobra for dinner seemed like a common occurrence, but Melvin had to smirk when he pictured the African trying to eat a coney island hot dog.

"Say, where did anyone ever get the idea to eat a snake?" It was Paul, drunken and patting the African's shoulder again.

The man seemed slightly startled, but he smiled graciously and answered, "You see, many of the peoples in my continent live primitively with virtually no contact from outsiders. Many of these cultures have had to be, as you may say, 'self-sufficient' in maintaining their existence."

Paul's intent gaze suggested that he was interested in the African's trivial story, yet Melvin knew that Paul had really wanted a short answer—not a history lesson. But, the African continued, "During many seasons the weather here is too unpredictable for adequate farming, however, our wildlife is abundant, especially snakes." The African paused for a sip of his drink. "Legends say that if a man eats a snake he will be protected from evil spirits."

Paul rolled his eyes. "Oh," he replied finishing another drink.

Paul was well on his way to over-doing it with the alcohol. Melvin also knew that he should not make an issue out of it either. Paul had the tendency to be one of those unpredictable drunks that could be laughing one minute and brawling with half the bar the next. Besides, Melvin was far too preoccupied with his own drink to worry about Paul.

Finally their drinking and thinking was interrupted by the disgusting bartender who flopped two plates in front of each of them and then hastily passed out their silverware.

"Cobra?" asked Paul who now looked squeamishly drunk.

"Yup," retorted the bartender chewing on a new toothpick.

Paul looked at Melvin, who was looking at Paul. It was time to eat and all of the Scotch in the bar would not make the difference now. In front of each of them was a large platter of deeply fried food sliced in large chunks that actually resembled cod fillets. In fact, the plate was even garnished with a piece of parsley and a slice of lemon. Melvin almost started to laugh at the garnishing for it was so unexpected it was silly considering the atmosphere of the smokey little tavern. He thought rationally. If he used his imagination perhaps he could convince himself that he was eating fish. Absently, he began pulling at the breading to look at the meat inside. It was whitish—like fish. He sighed, unnoticeable to anyone but him, for he half expected to see green meat peering at him from behind the crispy, golden breading. It seemed safe enough. He let his fork cut through the breaded chunk. The meat was flaky and seemed tender. Then, Melvin shovelled a small bite onto his fork, closed his eyes, and shoved the bite into his mouth. He chewed slowly, cautiously, at first and then more quickly, occasionally allowing the meat to bounce gingerly off of his taste buds. He swallowed. It was absolutely delicious. He stabbed the chunk again for another bite. This time it was a bigger one. Watching Melvin, Paul's confidence was boosted too, and upon swallowing his first bite, Paul began to giggle.

"This stuff is really good, Melvin."

Melvin just nodded for he was far too involved with his own meal.

Paul dove into his plate of cobra hungrily and did not look up until the plate was empty, which he celebrated with a loud, resounding belch that smelled slightly of Scotch. Melvin laughed at his friend now, slapped him on the shoulder, and said, "Hey, Paul, are you still hungry?". . . .

IX

Melvin Howard chuckled to himself and shook his head with the recollection. At that moment, as I watched Melvin Howard wipe a tear from his laughing eyes, I could not help hoping that some day I would be able to tell a funny story about one of my own experiences. I also wondered if I would ever be able to share anything with a friend as Melvin Howard had with Paul Cassini. For now, I kept this to myself because thinking this way made me feel pathetic, and I was afraid that Melvin Howard would see that in me too. Instead of speaking, I became courageous and raised the glass of grapefruit juice to my lips. This time when I sipped it flowed smoothly past my lips. My throat bobbed until I had swallowed the very last drop. After the last gulp I sighed and wiped my mouth on my shirt sleeve.

"I'll be," said Melvin Howard without emotion, but his eyes were wide and bright.

For some reason, that glass of grapefruit juice was no longer bitter, and I smiled back at Melvin Howard and at my reflection in his eyes.

Cleaning up Melvin Howard's basement was no easy chore for he was somewhat of a pack rat. It seemed like he had not thrown anything away in his life, and I just imagined times when my mother had insisted that I get rid of some of my things for Goodwill so it would be easier to reorganize my room. Melvin Howard's basement was the biggest clutter of disorganization that I had ever seen. In fact, I think the amount of things that Melvin Howard owned even surprised him. We rummaged through box after box, organizing and disorganizing current piles into new ones. Hidden in these boxes were many unique treasures that added visual effects to Melvin Howard's tales. Each newly discovered item prompted a different story from Melvin Howard too. I was so surprised by this because there were so many things, but this old man knew the history of each item, no matter how potentially useless or insignificant.

Gradually, the two of us gained an attrition of his belongings until we could comfortably stand in one corner. It was here that I stooped to heave a particularly heavy box. I could barely budge it. I tried again, centering most of my strength to lift the weight in my legs as I had learned in gym class. I got the box raised to my knees when just like that the bottom snapped open, dumping the contents onto the floor in a rush. Quickly Melvin Howard hopped over stuff to help me.

"That's all right," he said comfortingly even though I had not yet voiced my apology. Maybe, I did not have to. My face was aghast with humiliation and shock.

"I'm sorry."

Melvin Howard grabbed the broken cardboard from my clumsy fingers and patted my shoulder.

"It's okay," he said. "You made no mistake. It was an accident."

"Are you sure that I didn't break anything?"

"You broke nothing except your pride."

I cast my eyes downward in embarrassment and felt like I do when my father scolds me for doing something wrong.

"In the future," he continued softly, "you will know that you should get some help when things are too heavy."

I nodded, feeling better since there was no harm done. I just didn't want him to think I was unreliable, which his experienced eyes saw right through.

"Don't worry son, you don't need to impress me. That's one thing I've definitely grown too old for," said Melvin Howard giving my shoulder one last pat.

"C'mon help me pick these things up," he said.

With my confidence renewed I eagerly stooped and began sorting through the pile on the floor, organizing it into smaller, easier to handle boxes upon Melvin Howard's suggestion. This incident stuck with me as one of the finest lessons I have ever learned from Melvin Howard. For once, I learned, it was all right to be weak as long as I could be strong enough and smart enough to admit to my weakness.

While admiring Melvin Howard's wisdom and cleaning up the mess that for which I still felt responsible, I noticed Melvin Howard's attention had been diverted to the floor. He stared at a picture that he now picked up slowly in his right hand. It was an old black and white photograph of a woman. Despite the age of the picture I could tell that the woman was young at the time in which the photograph had been taken. She had fair and beautiful facial features. Whomever this woman was she definitely had invoked a memory from Melvin Howard for his eyes seemed to be lost and melancholy as he engrossed himself further in the photograph. Finally, he sighed wearily like a very old man, which seemed unfitting for him.

"My daughter," he said.

X

It was early on a Saturday in April when Melvin Howard heard the annoying "shave and a haircut. . ."-knock on his front door to indicate that Mark Austin had arrived to see his sixteen-year-old daughter, Janie. Reluctantly, Melvin Howard walked over to greet Mark at the door as much as he was wishing that it wouldn't be Mark. Just like many fathers, Melvin Howard's daughter had been his pride and joy. When she was growing up he had pampered her every chance he could, and through none of his doing, Janie grew up to be an exceptionally beautiful girl. From the time she had turned fourteen, it seemed that there were always boys stopping by to say 'hello'. Most of them were well-mannered young gentlemen that had set early, youthful goals. These boys were likeable to him because they treated Janie well and gave promise of being successful in adulthood.

Then one night after Janie and several friends had gone on a sledding party, she brought in a new boy to meet the scrutinizing "Mr. Howard", as all the boys so meekly addressed him. This boy was Mark Austin.

Mark came into the living room with Janie to meet Melvin Howard, who was engrossed in the sports page of The Blade. The Browns were getting blistered by the Raiders on a television set that only served as background to a typical early winter evening in Northwest Ohio. Melvin Howard put his paper down when he heard his daughter's sweet voice announce the latest suitor to him.

"Daddy, I want you to meet Mark Austin. Mark, this is my father." The last words Janie spoke seemed to mix in with the background noise of the television for Melvin Howard's full attention was now focused on the boy before him. He was clad in an olive drab U. S. Army jacket, frayed, grubby old blue jeans, and most noticeably, long brown hair that cascaded well past his shoulders.

The instinctive smile on Melvin Howard's face faded, and he withdrew his hand that instinctively accompanied his smile when meeting any of Janie's friends. Mark wasn't like any of the boys that Janie had previously brought over. Instantly, Melvin Howard was ashamed of himself for passing such an immediate judgment, but the boy's appearance made him uncomfortable and hesitant. Still, to appease Janie, Melvin Howard uttered a 'hello' and once more extended his hand to Mark Austin, who uncomfortably took it and said, "Nice to meet you, sir."

There was disquieting silence until Janie spoke up.

"Mark's a senior, Daddy."

Now, Melvin Howard found something to say. "A senior? Then, you'll be graduating this year?"

"Yes," replied Mark.

'Maybe it's because of the boy's long hair that makes it impossible to really see into his eyes,' thought Melvin Howard. "And, what do you intend to do after you graduate?" asked Melvin. This was usually the most important question Melvin Howard ever felt the need to quiz Janie's boyfriends with because their ambition in life beyond high school was what really mattered.

"I'm not sure, sir. That seems so far away." The boy's answer kicked Melvin Howard solidly as if it had been a provoked mule.

From that moment on, Melvin Howard's relationship with his daughter changed from one of trust and caring to turmoil and caution. Despite familial struggles, Janie kept seeing Mark, and Melvin Howard kept failing to understand the non-ambitious youth that his daughter dated.

Now, it was April and time for the Junior-Senior Prom at school. Naturally, Mark had asked Janie since they were considered to be "going steady." Melvin Howard, reluctantly agreed to his daughter attending the dance with Mark, for he still felt it was important to respect his daughter's judgment. After all, Janie seemed content with Mark, and Mark never seemed to mistreat her. So, Melvin Howard felt foolish entertaining thoughts of refusing Mark the chance to see Janie and gave the "okay" for her to go to the prom.

Now, Mark was waiting on the porch. Impatiently, he knocked again. Melvin Howard reluctantly walked across to the door, glancing out the peep hole before pulling it open to reveal a Mark Austin never before seen by Melvin Howard, or perhaps anyone else. Mark forced a hesitant smile and a wave. Melvin Howard did not return these gestures and mechanically opened the screen door for Mark to gain entrance. Dressed in a fine cream-colored tuxedo with a ruffled lavender shirt, bow tie, and transparently shined dress shoes, Mark stepped regally into the foyer.

"Hello, Mark," Melvin Howard finally said to the young man. "You look nice."

"Thanks, sir," managed Mark embarrassedly, blushing beneath his lengthy but trimmed and combed hair.

Then Melvin Howard, in spite of his feelings for Mark, did something he had not done since he met this surprising boy, he offered Mark his hand. This time Mark grasped Melvin Howard's hand and squeezed it firmly, legitimately smiling like the child on the playground who has just been accepted by his peers. 'Maybe,' thought Melvin Howard, 'there was some glimmer of hope for this boy after all.' What that hope was exactly Melvin Howard was still not quite sure; but at least, he decided that he would try to give Mark a fair chance. Perhaps he owed it to Mark to accept him. It wasn't hard to realize how happy Janie was around Mark, and for that reason alone, his daughter's happiness, was enough reason for Melvin Howard to be accepting.

"Where are you going besides the prom?" Even though Janie had been talking of their pre-, during, and post-prom plans for literally weeks, Melvin Howard felt it uncomfortably necessary to engage Mark in some sort of small talk.

"Well, sir," started Mark, "first we will be meeting some friends for dinner at the Wine Cellar."

The boy even spoke in a more dignified manner. 'Clothes certainly made the man,' thought Melvin Howard tritely.

"Then after the prom," Mark continued to make this officially the longest conversation that he and Melvin Howard had ever had, "some friends, the same ones we're having dinner with, are having a party—a small one," Mark added as if to placate his date's overly concerned father.

"Either way, I'll trust you to make sure Janie is home early and that she has a wonderful time," said Melvin Howard smiling with a new-found pride and trust.

"Oh yes, sir," said Mark nervously shaking Melvin Howard's hand for lack of a better reaction to the older man's obvious and unpredicted confidence.

Soon Janie came downstairs. She was beautiful in her satiny, billowing prom dress. Her hair had been stretched back into a bun and adorned with baby's breath. Out of the corner of his eye Melvin Howard caught a glimpse of Mark's worshipping gaze. He looked lovingly at Janie as she slowly made her descent down the staircase like an angel.

'Thank God,' thought Melvin Howard to himself. His daughter was a wonderful creation and suddenly the over-protective father felt the need to congratulate God on a job well done. In the same moment, Melvin Howard realized how much he loved his wife too, for together, with God, they had given life to Janie. No matter what other accomplishments he ever attained, Janie was by far the most special and any regrets were strictly impossible during that moment.

After posing for several photographs, Mark escorted Janie to his car; the perfect gentleman. Melvin Howard looked on proudly and he smiled so broadly and truly that a tear began to settle in the corner of his eye. As the tear of joy began to trickle down his cheek he reached out and embraced his wife. He loved his family.

XI

The telephone rang alarmingly in the middle of the night. The high-pitched tone shrieked two more times before Melvin Howard secured his senses enough to realize where he was. He was on his own living room couch and all of the lights had been turned out. He was waiting up for Janie, not to check up on her, but to let her know that he now approved of Mark. He also felt the urge to hug her and tell her that he loved her.

The phone rang again, and Melvin Howard grabbed up the receiver, still somewhat stupefied from having dozed off.

"Hello," yawned Melvin Howard.

"Mr. Howard?" asked a strange voice at the other end.

"Yes?"

"Mr. Howard, my name is John Calvin, I'm a police officer, and your daughter Janie has been involved in an accident. We will need you to come to the hospital, sir."

"What do you mean?" Melvin Howard was now wide awake. His mind had a million questions to ask, however, panic prevented him from creating logical sense of anything.

"Please sir, I can explain more when you arrive. Please come to St. Charles Hospital. We need you and your wife to come over immediately." The voice spoke professionally with a twinge of pain for each of the terrible words his job had now forced him to utter.

Melvin Howard was silent, fighting the tears, hoping for the best, expecting the worst.

"Mr. Howard?"

"Yes?" Melvin Howard choked out.

"Can you come?"

"Yes."

By the time Melvin Howard and his wife, Marcia had arrived at the hospital, the waiting area for the emergency room was crowded with people, all of which the Howards recognized as being the parents of Janie's friends.

One of the men there Melvin Howard recognized as Mark's father. Rather than waiting, he strode to the receptionist's desk.

"My name is Melvin Howard. We were told our daughter was here." He said more calmly than he had expected.

"Yes, she is in room 311," the chubby black nurse said with no concern, emotions icy from her job.

"May we see her?" asked Marcia. The concern, however, was very present in her voice.

"Yes, is she all right?" Melvin Howard asked confusedly.

"I'm sorry sir," the nurse said apologetically shaking her head, "but you'll need to wait with the others over there," she gestured toward the other parents.

"But. . . ."

"I'm sorry sir, but we have no information here. The doctor will be down shortly." the nurse interrupted.

After filling out a billing ledger and some proper insurance forms, Melvin and Marcia Howard walked zombie-like to join the other parents who knew as little as they did. Melvin Howard slumped into a chair beside his wife then quickly stood again. He was far too nervous and too ignorant of the current situation to sit and pretend to be relaxed. The rest of the parents were silent. Their faces were rock-hard with concern. No one cried and no one spoke. Mark's father sat bent over looking at the floor, clutching his hat in both hands. The air felt bad, and it was now far too easy to expect anything but the worst. It was agonizing to think that his daughter was here in the hospital and possibly struggling for her very life. All her life, Melvin and Marcia had been able to help Janie in her times of trouble. Now, separated from her, both of them were utterly powerless.

Melvin Howard sat again long enough to pat his wife's hand; however, he was soon back up again. He was restless and wanted to pace, but he successfully fought the urge to do so. He wanted to approach the desk to inquire as to the whereabouts of the doctor, yet he wanted to remain calm. He wanted to speak comfortingly to Mark's father, but he couldn't figure out what words should be said. Instead, Melvin Howard did nothing but suffer inside alone through this nightmare that was supposed to happen to 'someone else's kids'.

Finally, after an eternity of breaking in and out of cold sweats and being lost in complete thought, a gentle voice whispered in Melvin Howard's ear.

"The doctor's here, Melvin." It was his wife.

He looked up from the white tile floor that he had been staring at for what seemed like hours and briefly locked his eyes on Marcia's tear-stained face. She was a beautiful woman and always had been. Now, it was as if he saw her for the first time, recalling how in her youth, she had closely resembled Janie. Janie. Then everything began to register again. He tried to force a faked smile at his wife, but he was too confused to be happy about anything, even loving her. Regardless, the doctor was here now and maybe there would be good news. But, Melvin Howard also realized that the news might not be good. Either way, he decided that this would be better than being totally in the dark.

The doctor stood before him extending his hand. "My name is Dr. Nowak," he said. Dr. Nowak, a name Melvin Howard was sure he would never forget.

"Mr. and Mrs. Howard, please come with me." Dr. Nowak spoke cordially, but it was obvious that long, toiling hours in the emergency room had broken down this doctor's hospitality.

"May we see our daughter?" inquired Marcia. She had always been so very positive, and Melvin was certain he couldn't bear to see her otherwise.

"First, Mrs. Howard, I need to talk to you and your husband privately," replied Dr. Nowak.

The Howards followed Dr. Nowak into one of the several conference rooms just off of the emergency area. Once inside the three of them were seated. Then there was a long silence. Dr. Nowak seemed to be catching his breath. Once again, Melvin Howard noticed how bad the air felt. His stomach turned rambunctious awaiting the doctor's words, which were now greater than God.

"Mr. and Mrs. Howard," Dr. Nowak now began slowly.

"Yes?" replied Melvin Howard nervously before the doctor could continue.

"These incidents, as you might know, are most difficult for me. Seeing young people involved in such a terrible situation hurts me deeply because, I too, am a father," he sighed apologetically, searching their eyes for support.

"Before I go on, I want you to know that Janie and her friends were involved in a serious accident. They crashed head-on into a semi and then their car rolled over a couple times. Officer Calvin can tell you more of those types of details; however, my job requires that I explain the outcomes of such accidents." The doctor paused long enough to remove his glasses and rub his eyes. "Your daughter, Mr. and Mrs. Howard," the doctor sighed desperately searching for a way to be gentle, "suffered a serious head wound as well as massive internal bleeding as a result of the accident. I'm sorry."

The words "I'm sorry" began to echo painfully in Melvin Howard's ears. He then fixed his gaze squarely on the doctor, who carefully planned his next set of words. Dr. Nowak swallowed hard as if he had eaten a brick and then in the same breath he spit out his words.

"The internal damage was too great. She lost too much blood. I'm sorry," the doctor again struggled and paused as if he were losing his breath. But, Melvin Howard, with his eyes already heavily laden with tears, had clearly decided that he had heard enough and did not want to hear any more. Then, Dr. Nowak said it. "There was nothing we could do." There was no gentle way to say it because no matter what, Melvin and Marcia Howard's young daughter, Janie was dead.

. . . Melvin Howard sat for what seemed to be a very long time staring blankly at the picture. His forehead was furrowed with sadness and pain I had never experienced. He was obviously reminiscing about her, but this time, I knew that Melvin Howard would keep his memories to himself. At that moment, Melvin Howard proved to me that even the strongest, most positive people can be lost and lonely. The rest of the basement could wait.

XII

A good week went by before I saw Melvin Howard again. It was Saturday and I showed up to help him out around the house as we had originally arranged. During that week, several times, I entertained the idea of visiting him; however, I felt awkward visiting him without a proper invitation. After all, he was an adult and probably busy. I was a seventh grader who had no real friends my age. I did not want to be a pest. So, I held off my visitation until Saturday when I was certain we could continue in our pursuit of cleaning up his basement.

I had honestly been looking forward to the weekend too because school had become worse than ever. Like many teenagers, seventh grade was tough for me because it seemed that there was so much pressure. In my case, this pressure presented itself as physical abuse by the other boys in the phys. ed. locker room, complete rejection by any of the girls, even the ones who themselves were rejected, and the constant disappointment that was directed toward me by my teachers. Unfortunately, I was also climbing into a desperate position, to which I had been somewhat ignorant. I was currently failing four of my seven subjects, and my parents, who had grown accustomed to my low grades now became very concerned. If I continued at my current pace, I would surely be held back to try seventh grade again. My parents reviewed my progress reports even as I walked to Melvin Howard's. I was glad I would be able to escape their scrutiny for a few hours, but the part that was critical to me was the discussion that I was sure they were having. They would feel the need to punish me for my irresponsibility, and I knew that one of the things they could easily hang over my head was my Saturday afternoon jobs with Melvin Howard; which little did they know had become the greatest learning experience I had ever known.

When Melvin Howard met me at the door he was the same enthusiastic pillar of confidence and strength that I had now come to know.

"Martin!" he exclaimed. "It certainly is great to see you today."

At this I smiled and followed his gesture into the house. I was certainly glad to see that he was feeling better than when I had last seen him.

Before we started in on the basement again, Melvin Howard invited me into his rustic family room to have, what would become for us a tradition, an ice cold glass of grapefruit juice. This time, realizing that its bitterness was not so bad, I took a healthy gulp and didn't even wince when the after taste hit. It still wasn't my favorite beverage; however, I no longer hated it.

"So, Martin, how's school?" Melvin Howard inquired.

Immediately I thought, 'Not him too!' With pressure like this from everywhere I certainly would not survive until high school, much less college, as my parents were expecting. Having to fight a two front war was what killed Germany in World War II, and it would seriously kill me as well.

"Hmm, I sense tension here."

Apparently, my own thoughts had delayed my answer long enough for Melvin Howard to realize my restraint.

"School isn't going so hot, eh?" asked Melvin Howard trying his best to squeeze my feelings out of me.

"Not really sir."

"Why not?"

"I'm not sure," I answered. I did not know where to begin: my plight with the grades, which was my fault, or the rejection by my peers, which could not be helped because I found that teenagers are socially stubborn, and I had no chance of changing them.

"Don't worry, Martin; seventh grade is tough for every kid," he said philosophically gazing into another one of his especially warm and soothing fires.

His comment forced a nod out of me, merely to let him know that I was acknowledging his statement of advice; yet I was sure that I really didn't understand it or I did not actually believe it. First of all, I had a difficult time seeing Melvin Howard as a seventh grader—ever. Even though, I knew that he had obviously been a seventh grader at one time, I still could not picture him at my age because he seemed so knowledgeable and seasoned to have toyed with anything as fundamental as seventh grade. Secondly, I had a tough time believing that Larry Osterman and Jimbo Murray ever felt the same pressures of early adolescence as I was feeling. After all, those two guys were socially adjusted since girls, pretty ones, liked to talk to them. They had conquered puberty and were already growing patchy sprouts of whiskers under their chins, and to top everything off they were consistently on the honor roll.

"It's true, you know?" Melvin Howard asked.

He then got up to throw more crumbled newspapers onto the fire. "Kids always love to pick on whoever is weakest in their eyes. It's part of being a kid. Doesn't mean it's exactly right, but it is all part of becoming socialized as a human being. Some kids get all the breaks when they're young, especially the ones that grow early; but it's the 'late bloomers' who seem to really profit later on." He was standing before me now and his shadow from

55

.

the firelight was cast gigantic against the wall, so large that it out-sized the allegedly record-setting marlin.

"Why?" I asked even though I felt my mind wandering around the room, observing everything.

Nevertheless, Melvin Howard's answer came straightforward and loud, not angry but emphatic; thus rousing me from my own thoughts and once again wresting my attention back into place. "Because 'late bloomers' have at one time or another been picked on by the other kids who seem to be growing up quickly."

I shriveled my brow only half accepting his words, which he noticed immediately and went on.

"Martin, you're not a freak of nature! They are," he said like a football coach trying to pep up his losing team at halftime. "You see, seventh graders were meant to be kids, not men. So, the ones that take their time growing up are actually following nature's plan. Trust me, you will catch up one day."

"Until then what should I do?" I asked.

"Just ignore them or try to become friends with them through your own strengths. I'm sure you have some."

He was probably right, I felt, even though I was not exactly sure what my strengths were; or if I even had any at all. Plus, I had difficulty understanding his concept of "ignoring them". The only thing I was thoroughly convinced of was that ignoring Jimbo and Larry while they gave me a first-rate "wedgie" would be next to impossible.

Melvin Howard stepped back over to his easy chair and sat down on the edge of it, took a short sip of his grapefruit juice, and then spoke.

"Let me tell you a little story, Martin. Are you interested?"

"Yes, sir," I answered quickly trying not to be too anxious because I truly loved these stories of his and was beginning to look forward to hearing a new one each time I visited.

"All right then. Whether you can believe it or not, I was also a seventh grader once," he laughed slightly. "I was also a 'late bloomer'." "When I was a seventh grader I wanted very much to play on the school basketball team. I was not a poor athlete, but basketball, honestly, was not my best suit. This was true especially because. . . "

XIII

Melvin Howard stepped onto the floor with many other seventh grade boys. It was three o'clock, school was out, and the other kids were well on their way home or stopping off at the candy store. But, the candy store would have to wait for Melvin Howard and the rest of these boys, hopefully months, for they were anxiously in pursuit of a dream. The climb to becoming a star on the high school varsity team began here in seventh grade. Here thirty-five underdeveloped and gangling boys would be first, cut down to a workable roster of fourteen. Then, slowly but surely, with hope, encouragement, and military-style hard work they would be molded and nurtured into a competitive unit that would leave the school with an enviable and wondrous tradition.

Coaches, however, had a difficult job because among the boys on the floor there wasn't one that didn't have the necessary desire to play. Skills would be the tell-tale sign as they always were for who got cut and for who made the team. Sometimes, particular players were recognized as having potential for growth as a ball player and were allotted a position on the team with hopes that they could become talented.

But, for now, every boy, including Melvin Howard felt he was, by far, the most skilled athlete on the floor. Many of the others were busy shooting jump shots way out of their range or were engaged in awkward scrimmages where fouls seemed to be the main objective because they occurred more often than baskets. Melvin Howard, however, felt confident but nervous, so he was content to just stand idly in the gym for a few moments, allowing the initial jitters to subside. While standing off to the side with basketballs rebounding recklessly all around him, Melvin Howard crossed his thin arms across his juvenile chest and thought. He was imagining himself far beyond this first parctice. No, instead, Melvin Howard, imagined himself trying to ignore the chanting, noisy, hometown crowd as he stepped up to the foul line clad in the visiting green jersey of his varsity team. With only two seconds remaining in the game to decide the sectional champion, Melvin Howard had come off the bench (since real heroes never seemed to start) to score twenty points in his team's amazing come-from-behind effort that now had them only trailing by one. But, that one point might as well be a million if Melvin Howard was unable to sink these two critical free throws. He had to hit at least one shot to insure a tie and overtime; but he was confident and settling for just one made shot was utterly out of the question. It was "do or die", Melvin Howard thought as he stepped to the line. He wiped the sweat from his palms and took the ball from the official. "Concentrate," he told himself eyeing the orange rim that stood alone, out from the hostile, hometown crowd that lurked behind it. Their chanting grew even louder, literally hoisting the rafters of the gymnasium. But, right now, for Melvin Howard there could be no crowd, friendly or hostile, just an orange, iron rim. The rim was empty. He could fix that. The ball left his hand crisply and it spun high until it started its gentle descent, still spinning as if it were a planet out of orbit. Then just as crisply as it had left his hot hand, the ball snapped through the nylon meshing to tie the game. The crowd erupted instantly with a loud mixture of cheers and boos. Melvin Howard quickly glanced at the scoreboard, which now indicated a tie. He still was too intent to smile and his job was not yet finished.

The referee handed him the basketball again. Concentration was the key here. With it, he would be a hero and his team would reign supreme as sectional champs. Without it, the game would probably go into overtime, once again, making it either team's ball game.

Young Melvin Howard rotated the basketball slightly in his hands to find the comfort that he had found on his first shot. He eyed the rim from behind the ball, now positioned for flight. In his mind he again imagined the ball sliding over the front lip of the orange iron, through the basket, and to the floor below. Melvin Howard then pushed the ball toward the hoop. Spinning perfectly and straight, the ball arched toward the rim. Eyes wide with excitement, Melvin Howard watched his second and most critical foul shot drop cleanly through the net to make his team sectional champs. The crowd was silent, but his teammates had him hoisted to their shoulders, chanting and yelling —the most glorious feeling Melvin could ever hope to feel.

Now, with a smile fixed to his lips he stepped onto the floor with the rest of the seventh grade hopefuls. It all started here. Promptly, Melvin jumped in and rebounded the forced shot of another young player. After properly coming down with the ball, Melvin Howard turned and fired a shot off the backboard. The shot, however, was hurried and clumsy; so off of the glass it came with the inertia of a rocket at take off.

"Brick!" yelled two of the other boys. Melvin Howard scowled even though he was more embarrassed than angry. After all, they merely called the shot as they had seen it. He would have to work on his touch, then he would show those other guys.

Finally after several more minutes of rebounding and trying to shoot, the coach walked in. He was the stereotypical coach wearing coaching shorts and a tennis shirt that was snug over his huge belly. At one point in his life, the coach probably was a very strong athlete; however, it was clear now that he seldom exercised and usually drank a lot of beer. Still, this coach, Mr. Brummer, by name, was supposed to be a knowledgeable coach and a good role model for the kids who played for him. Coach Brummer was not supposed to be a soft-spoken man but for now he said nothing. He just watched, studying the boys on the floor, who were now very eager to show off their best stuff in hopes that the coach would take primary notice of each one of them as a possible star.

Then, with a sharp blast of a whistle the shooting stopped. "Okay, gentlemen, place the balls on the floor over there," Coach Brummer said pointing to the far wall, "and then line up along this wall," to which he gestured also.

The boys obeyed and were quickly in line after placing the balls in their designated area. Their enthusiasm brought a smile to the chubby coach's face as he looked them over and then began carefully.

"Three things that I'm going to look for in the next couple days are: One," he emphasized this by holding up his index finger, "attitude. Two, an understanding of the basic game skills. And three, the ability to always give 100% effort to teamwork."

Unfortunately, for Melvin Howard and several of the others these words just washed over. He was too anxious to begin. He was too anxious to start shooting and rebounding. He wanted to be impressive and for now that was all he could think of.

After the coach's brief pep talk, the boys were split into two lines for a lay-up drill. One line rebounded and passed while the other received the pass and made the lay-up off the backboard. Melvin Howard found himself in the lay-up line, about the third boy down and so far the boys were making their lay-ups, but it was now Melvin Howard's turn. He concentrated hard. He too was going to make the lay-up. Melvin was intent when he saw Kirby O'Neil come down with the rebound, dribble once, and fire the pass. Melvin, however, was so intent on making the shot that he simply forgot about one particular skill necessary for making the lay-up—catching the ball. Melvin's concentration on the shot was there, but the ball slipped right through his hands, forcing him to chase after it. Once he got hold of the basketball, Melvin Howard was flustered, and the lay-up ricocheted off the bottom of the rim. He had definitely made an impression, for all eyes were on him, especially Coach Brummer's.

The young, ambitious Melvin Howard was so frustrated and embarrassed by his feeble attempt that it was all he could do to hustle back to the line.

"Howard!" yelled Coach Brummer. The coach's loud voice shook Melvin from his daze.

"Yes, sir."

"You're in the wrong line."

It was true. Melvin was standing in the lay-up line again when the correct rotation would have meant for him to switch over to the rebounding line. The eyes were on him again, and he was sweating nervously.

"Sorry, sir."

"Don't apologize. Just get over to the right line."

Melvin immediately dashed over to the other line and stood there wishing he could cower from the gaze of his peers. He had to regain his concentration so that he would not commit any more foolish errors. He would get a good strong rebound here to hopefully renew the coach's confidence in him as a player.

Mike Flaherty made his lay-up, and Melvin Howard made the rebound successfully. This time Kirby O'Neil would be receiving Melvin's pass. The pass needed to be good; but it wasn't. Instead of a nice crisp chest pass as was Melvin Howard's intention, he threw it too hard and too high. The ball sailed over Kirby's head and bounced off of a wall behind the rest of the team. From there, the ball continued to bounce until it finally stopped against the wall on the far side of the gym.

"Howard, go get that basketball, please," said Coach Brummer. The coach's patience seemed to be waning.

The rest of the practice went just as miserably. Melvin was sure that Coach Brummer would not be convinced that he was an adequate ball player now no matter what. This newly-gained, self-defeating attitude mixed with frustration carried into the next day of practice to the point where Melvin was sure that the others secretly laughed at him. By the third and final day of try-outs, Melvin walked disparagingly into the locker room. Three days before he was enthusiastic about building a dream to be a basketball hero. Today, however, Melvin considered the idea of practice drudgery and a waste of time. He still knew that his first day of floundering through drill after drill had definitely set the precedent for his future as a basketball player.

That last day, Melvin Howard slumped and sulked his way through the entire practice, making clumsy, obvious mistakes, and feeling morally tortured the whole time. At the end of practice the coach called the boys to gather at the middle of the floor. While Coach Brummer gave a standard speech about 'all the players trying hard and how he as coach would have a tough decision to make concerning the final cuts,' Melvin hid in the shadows of the other boys. His excited, hopeful smile that was fixed confidently to his face just three days ago had disappeared. He was now shy and nonchalant. In fact, the only thing Melvin decided he wanted now was a quick escape from the voiceless, yet ridiculing eyes of his peers.

The coach said, "Final cuts will be posted on the bulletin board in the library before school starts. If you find your name on the list then you need to report tomorrow afternoon to the gym for practice because that means you will be a part of the team." Melvin felt the strange desire to be absent from school the next day.

The next day came and despite desiring otherwise, Melvin Howard was in school the next day. Luckily, he showed because his social studies teacher gave a pop quiz, on which to his amazement, he got an "A." But, it was already third period, and Melvin had not checked the bulletin board in the library yet for Mr. Brummer's final list of ball players. At this point, in fact, he wasn't so sure he wanted to check the list. Like the quiz he just "aced," he already knew the answer to the personal question: "Did I make the team?" Nevertheless, he also was sure that he would check the list out of sheer curiosity to see what boys did make the team.

Melvin Howard, hesitantly made his way through the halls to the library where he found the list of names. The list itself was not impressive at all. Fourteen names neatly printed onto a yellow legal sheet in blue ink, probably thin line marker. The names were listed alphabetically, so it was easy for Melvin Howard to confirm his previous beliefs.

"Evers, Flaherty, Garrison, Henry, Lowry, Meyers," read Melvin silently but moving his lips as each name registered in his young brain. Regardless of how he read these names they all spelled out the same thing to young Melvin Howard. He was rejected. He read all the way through the list to see if maybe the coach did not put his name at the bottom of the list as an afterthought, however, it was not there. This year the team would play without Melvin Howard. In a twisted sense, the young man wished for this team to be pitiful. This was the only true jealousy he let on to. Additionally, he already planned to give basketball another go as an eighth grader. . . .

"So, sir did you ever make the team?" I said still not inspired.

"No," he said flatly. "But, by George, I tried out every year until I graduated. I'm still not sure what possessed me to go through that so often." Melvin Howard forced a laugh and shook his head.

"Did you ever play any sports though?" I said. I was interested in sports even though I displayed little talent in any of them.

"Yes, I did," said Melvin Howard rekindling his pride. "That was my next point to show you that you have to find your strengths to be successful." He paused and looked at me. "Even though I always entertained thoughts of being a basketball hero," he said. "Martin, I was interested in other sports too like baseball, football, and swimming."

I nodded.

"All of these sports held a fascination for me, but the sport I truly shined in was golf. I'm not sure why either, except that each time I played, each hole was different. The game requires concentration and it can be played in a relaxed manner or in a competitive vein. But, I would say the variety in each outing was the thing that made golf so wonderful."

Golf. This was not difficult to understand either for Melvin Howard was an old man, and I had often associated golf with checkers and other stereotypical retired persons' activities.

"I learned to play during my second summer with Harold D. Owens. He took me himself," beamed Melvin Howard proudly. "We went to a small par three where after Mr. Owens showed me some basic tips, I picked the game up immediately. I've played ever since." Melvin Howard finished and pointed to several trophies on a book shelf.

I had seen the trophies before but never really paid close attention to them. In total there were six trophies, each one was topped off with a cast metal golfer in mid-swing, and each one was shiny and completely free of dust. I found this ironic since the end tables in the same room were littered perpetually with peanut shells.

Melvin Howard walked over to the shining row of awards and picked one of them up carefully and read the engraving to me—"AAU State Runner-Up," said Melvin Howard reminiscently. "This was my first one," he said handing the trophy to me for a closer look. I cradled it carefully, not wanting to tarnish the award's silvery surface with my fingerprints.

"I was just seventeen when I won that one," said Melvin Howard. He had come over to sit beside me. He held another trophy. This one was gold. "This one, I received two years later just after my high school graduation."

I took this one from him too and looked at it admirably. The engraving this time read: "AAU State Champion."

"I'm very impressed, sir," I said not wanting to sound patronizing.

"The others are all from later tournaments," continued Melvin Howard. "But, these are the two that I am most proud of. Because of these two trophies, I was able to get these other ones."

"Could you teach me to play golf, sir?"

"Well, I can try Martin." His tone wasn't inspirational but kind. "After all, the only way that you can discover your strengths is by trying many things."

I smiled weakly.

"You may not find golf to be your cup of tea though just because I did."

"I understand," I replied carefully. I really did understand, especially since my major goal was not to be a good golfer but to be good at anything.

"Something my father used to tell me," chimed Melvin Howard confidently. "Success comes from success."

I squinted, confused. He went on, "If you focus on your talents, other things more or less fall into place."

This statement got me thinking. 'What was I good at?' I realized too that I might actually be in for quite an adventure trying to discover just what my talents were, but I didn't tell Melvin Howard this because I was afraid of seeming negative.

"This summer, we'll hit the links, Martin for a little golf," said Melvin Howard jubilantly.

XVI

The thought of Melvin Howard teaching me to play golf would normally be seen by most others as inconsequential with me passing all my subjects to get promoted to eighth grade. However, the thought of golfing seemed to be a much better choice as opposed to spending the good months of summer cooped up in a classroom trying to pass all of the courses I could not pass during the school year. So, the promise of golf lessons with Melvin Howard proved to be great motivation for me. While I was not ready to be given the Rhode's Scholarship for Academic Achievement, my grades did improve immensely, and I surprisingly began to learn in the classroom which I had not been able to do virtually all of my young life.

In fact, I kept the first test paper I received back after the idea of golfing with Melvin Howard. It was an English test over phrases and clauses, on which I received a "B", the highest mark I had ever gotten. I still have the paper, for this one test marks somewhat of a rebirth—the day Martin Hovrick became motivated. That May not only were my teachers pleased but my parents were pleased also. I came home with three "B's" and four "C's". Not great; but this report card was a motion in the right direction for me. I think those grades hung on our refrigerator for the entire summer. I never grew tired of looking at them either. One day, I even secretly imagined that there would be an "A" on the next one. Somehow I had opened a whole new area of possibilities.

It was early June, and I was out of school for the summer when Melvin Howard first took me golfing with him. Just as he had begun with Harold D. Owens, Melvin Howard took me to a par three where he felt that I would stand less of a chance of becoming discouraged because the holes were shorter and easier.

When we arrived at the course, we went into a cubbyhole of a room that was called the "pro shop" to pay. Melvin Howard allowed me to use his second set of clubs that consisted of five irons, two woods, and a putter. This was fortunate because it saved on renting them from the pro shop.

"One of the most difficult things about playing golf, Martin," said Melvin Howard. "Is paying for it."

Before we got to the first tee, Melvin Howard took some time out to explain some of the basic skills to me. He first showed me how to hold the club and how to keep my arm straight when swinging the club. Next, he showed me how to keep my head down, and how to always watch the ball during my shot. He said by keeping my head down with my eyes focused on the ball I would hit the ball more solidly. I tried several practice swings with him then Melvin Howard said, "Hands-on training is one of the best ways to learn."

With that we carried our clubs to the first tee. My first round of golf was about to begin and quite honestly I was nervous. I wanted to do well for Melvin Howard and for myself. So, I was busily rushing all the information through my memory that Melvin Howard had just told me.

Melvin Howard teed off first and since the course was only a par three he selected a five iron for the first hole. "Martin, remember that in this game, more important than power is just making solid contact with the ball," he said as he hovered over the ball, focusing his concentration squarely on it. "By making solid contact, your shot will be more accurate. Golf is a game for thinking men, so accuracy is more important than hitting the ball hard."

Now, I had this information to install in my memory too. It was inevitable, confusion would take over in the long run. But, rather than worrying about my problems, I watched Melvin Howard. He brought his club back straight and dropped it toward the teed-up golf ball with the same fluidity as before. The five iron's face smacked solidly against the ball lifting it high into the air. Eventually the ball fell back to earth one hundred and seventy yards away on the green. It looked incredibly easy, and now it was my turn to try.

"Just relax," said Melvin Howard. "Relax and concentrate."

I stood over the ball, trying to remember everything Melvin Howard had shown me earlier. I was using the three iron because Melvin Howard told me that until I got used to driving I should use a longer club. I agreed ignorantly since I really wasn't aware of what difference the clubs really made. Still, I tried my best to concentrate. I focused squarely on the ball. However, I neglected keeping my head down. I practically missed the ball for it only rolled about ten yards, and I took a huge "divot" that actually flew much further than the ball. I was stunned. Melvin Howard made it look easy.

"That's all right," chuckled Melvin Howard. "My first time out I hit a tree, and the ball actually bounced behind the tee somewhere."

I forced a smile.

"Besides you're here to learn and here is one of the greatest lessons to be learned from a round of golf. Golf teaches you to laugh at yourself. So, laugh when you can because it makes the game that much more fun," said Melvin Howard patting me on the back. I smiled easily now, walked ten yards, and played my second shot, which was not much better.

In fact, I laughed so often that first time golfing that I was afraid someone observing me would want to have me committed. My score was not good. Even still, I had enjoyed myself immensely and could not wait to try the game again. Melvin Howard even allowed me to keep his second set of clubs the rest of the week to practice. He figured that I could do some work on my chip shots in my own backyard. He also gave me some plastic golf balls so I would not break windows in the neighborhood.

That evening at supper, I could not stop talking about my afternoon golfing with Melvin Howard. My parents were amazed since they had not seen me so excited about anything in a long time. They were happy for me and they said so. But, even if they hadn't, their genuine feelings of sharing my excitement glowed in their faces. I was warmed with pride throughout my whole body. So, as soon as supper was over, and I had helped my mother clear the table, I excused myself and adjourned to the backyard with the nine iron in hand. I spent the rest of evening until sundown practicing my chip shots. I chopped one of the little plastic balls across the yard, followed it, and then chopped it back again. My shots seemed to improve just by the end of my practice. This improvement was mostly due to the fact that I wanted to improve so much that any improvement was easy to see. Melvin Howard had said we could play again the following week, and I was looking forward to what would eventually begin to be a regular part of my schedule.

XV

The next day I had to mow the grass at home, a chore which I always grumbled about. I mowed the grass at Melvin Howard's too usually, but I never complained about mowing his yard. Perhaps since Melvin Howard paid me for my work efforts I found less to complain about. At home, mowing the grass was purely my duty as the only teenager of the home. Even though the mower that I had been struggling with since I was ten-years-old was getting less difficult to push, I still was faced with trying to mow the grass through reddened, watery eyes. One of the many things I was allergic to was grass, so cutting the lawn tended to bring these allergies out in force. Despite the allergies, my mother never recognized my ailment as being a suitable reason for anyone else to do the yard but me. So, with reddened eyes and a runny nose I would push the mower, lifting and heaving it around tree trunks, bouncing it over roots, and occasionally stalling it in some very high weeds that always grew in one section of our yard.

After the mowing always came the worst part—raking the clippings; which was another plus for doing the mowing for Melvin Howard because he had a mower that bagged all of the clippings. At my house, however, mowing the grass and then raking all the clippings could sometimes take virtually all afternoon. Usually the length of this chore was due to my own laziness. I often would stop to loiter in between strokes of the rake wishing that some imaginary force would secretly arrive to help me whisk away the rest of the grass that was strewn across every inch of our yard.

While I slumped on the rake handle, taking my time, my mother would often yell out from the living room window, "Martin, you had better be finished with the yard by the time your father comes home." Then, very diligently, I would start raking since the yard had to be finished by the time my father came home. To this day, I'm not really sure just what my mother's threat involved though because the yard was always finished before my father came home.

Working thanklessly like this without pay always made me think of a Paul

Newman movie I had seen once on late night TV called "Cool Hand Luke." Luke was the hardest worker in a prison chain gang, but no matter what, Luke always got to do the most work. Through all of his hard work, Luke's attitude remained positive and hopeful even though the wardens tried their best to break him down. Eventually Luke gave in when he was forced to dig his own grave. Sometimes I would even take off my shirt and work extra hard, pretending to be Cool Hand Luke. Strangely enough, when I played this little game the work always got finished quicker. I would then come into the house sweaty with pieces of grass stuck to my frail arms, sniffing from my allergies to announce to my mother that the yard was 'finished before my father had returned home.' Then, consistently, she would tell me to wash up and to put on a clean shirt and that there was Kool-Aid in the refrigerator, which was always the case during the hot summer months at my house.

Today was different though. I had just poured myself a tall refreshing glass of lime flavored Kool-Aid, my favorite, when my mother popped back into the kitchen.

"Martin?"

I turned to face her, even though, I kept guzzling the Kool-Aid.

"Do you suppose you could go over and mow Mrs. McDaniel's yard?"

I was silent, except for the ice cube I was now chewing on. I wanted to say no, but my mother's line of questioning here meant that she had already told Mrs. McDaniel she would send me down right after I finished doing our yard.

"Well," I started.

"Good," said my mother as if she were relieved. "It's good, Martin that you help that dear old woman so often."

Mrs. McDaniel was indeed old but dear was definitely an entirely different story. In reality she was the most crotchety human being I have had the displeasure of meeting. In addition, to her irritable personality, she was also very critical of my work, which never pleased her. Plus, she rarely, if ever, paid me. Once I complained to mother about Mrs. McDaniel not paying me for my work; just once. Right after I had finished complaining my mom launched into an extended yet vibrant lecture about how I should be ashamed for wanting to take advantage of a poor, unfortunate old woman. So, Mrs. McDaniel had me cut her grass for free and my mother encouraged her to the point where the only one that ever felt taken advantage of was me.

Since Mrs. McDaniel did not own a lawn mower, I had to bring our stubborn relic that would once again force me into an afternoon of toiling with the rake to clean up the clippings. By the time I got to Mrs. McDaniel's house, she was standing on the porch scowling.

"You're late, Martin," she snarled.

My already poor attitude about this job got officially worse then. After all, I had come down as soon as I could. Right then, I felt like the only reason for me to live was to mow this woman's yard. I wanted to, for once, to tell her not to treat me so badly since I was doing her a favor.

"Sorry, Mrs. McDaniel. I was just finishing our yard when you phoned my mother," I sheepishly rationalized the wrong-doing that I had not even done. On the outside I was genuinely sorry; however, on the inside I was cursing her angrily.

"Well, Martin, we don't have time to converse," she said which was just fine by me. "After you mow the grass, of course you were planning on raking the yard too." Naturally, she had not seen the rake I was carrying as plain as day. "Good," she continued finally spotting the rake and pointing at it with an arthritically crooked index finger. Secretly, I felt like Dorothy locked in the tower by the Wicked Witch of the West watching the hour glass that indicated the time that Dorothy had yet to be alive. Dorothy had the ruby slippers, and the witch wanted them. There would be no deals or compromises. Only this old witch wanted her yard cut. The yard was large, the grass was high, and the sun was scorching, and I knew there would be no deals. I would work hard for no payment as usual. "When the yard is raked," said Mrs. McDaniel, "I want you to trim around the hedges and put my sprinkler out. Cutting the grass on a hot day like this can kill the whole yard."

I just nodded even though I now felt as if the idea to cut her yard had actually been mine and that she could care less as to whether or not I cut it at all. In fact, I almost apologized.

"Well, go on. Get busy!" she shrieked waving a limp, wrinkly hand at me that snapped loosely at the wrist.

I had no idea how old she was, but I was pretty sure she was the oldest person I had ever met. If I ever live as long as Mrs. McDaniel I think I should want to be extremely happy to be given the chance to enjoy life so long. Mrs. McDaniel, however, never seemed happy. She seemed to hate life and everything about it. Oddly enough, in that instant, I put my anger toward her aside because, in truth, I felt sorry for her. I wanted so badly to ask her why she was so unhappy and what could make her happy again. I was concerned, yet I did not want to be, which allowed me to direct some of my anger inward to myself.

"Well?" she stood upon the porch scolding me, pointing her gnarled index finger again. With each point, her finger seemed to cut into my insides. Goodness she was cruel. Now, however, I wasted no more time. Instead, I positioned the mower and pulled the cord straight and quick. Then after a simultaneous re-adjustment of the choke the engine ignited and charged life into the mower. I gave an uncomfortable wave to Mrs. McDaniel who was still standing up on her porch. I could feel her eyes burning critical holes into various parts of my body. She always watched me work, and I hated it because she was always ready to pounce on me for every little error that I might commit. In fact, she even invented errors from time to time.

My nerves reacted cooperatively with the blazing sun rays till I was sweating so profusely that my T-shirt was soaked. I wanted to stop to take my shirt off, but by stopping, Mrs. McDaniel would think that I was slacking off and verbally lash out at me 'to get back to work.' Out of the corner of my eye I could see she was still standing on the porch, firm and tyrannical. The anger that I had originally felt crept back.

The whole job of cutting Mrs. McDaniel's yard took over two hours because she had me rake the front twice. After I had finished the first time she felt that there were still far too many clippings left on the grass. The second raking was the hardest work I've done in some time because I couldn't find anything to rake. But, I still tried anyway just to make Mrs. McDaniel happy; if that was even possible.

At the end of my slaving, Mrs. McDaniel finally said, "Thank you," a comment that was neither encouraging nor obligatory; but rather it was stated merely because she felt that she had to say something. Likewise, I had plenty to say but I found no way to voice any of these insulting remarks my mind was creating. So, for lack of anything better to say I answered simply, "You're welcome." I hope she did not see me bite my lip. No matter, for once again, I was not paid for my laboring. I stood momentarily leaning on my rake sweating a river from my brow and underarms. My allergies had my sinuses blocked solid, and Mrs. McDaniel still stood before me. She wasn't smiling at all, and she was not going to acknowledge my good deed with even a sincere thank you much less payment. Suddenly the image of Cool Hand Luke flashed before me again. This image of Cool Hand Luke is the only excuse I can even give for what I did next. Just like Cool Hand Luke, I wanted to be released from my sufferage (even though mine was exaggerated compared with his). With all of the anger welling up inside of me, I slammed the rake to the ground and asked the old woman, half-screaming at her, "Aren't you going to pay me?" She just stared, except for her mouth that had instantly dropped open when my insolent question bounced off her ears. She was speechless. I, however, was not, so I went on. In fact, I was starting to feel a twinge of warm, clever smugness.

"You never really pay me," I said trying not to smile in spite of myself.

"But. . . . ," squeaked Mrs. McDaniel. Her surprise grew simultaneously with my courage.

"You don't!" I had regained my intended anger now. Then in one quick motion I snatched up the rake, jerked the lawn mower around, and started for home. "I don't want to mow your lawn ever again!" I shouted over my shoulder before I trudged off trying to stay angry while part of me wanted to do handsprings knowing that crotchety, old Mrs. McDaniel was still standing on her porch speechless. I had done what probably every kid that had ever lived on her street had wanted to do. I was planning to relish in this personal victory for a long time. The only thing that actually depressed me was that I really wanted some friends to tell my tale to. Then suddenly my depression left me for Melvin Howard popped into my mind. I would tell Melvin Howard.

XVI

When I arrived at Melvin Howard's door he was reading a Sports Illustrated in front of the air conditioner. I was out of breath because I had run the whole way. I could see him sitting there across the house, and I must have scared him when I knocked because he jumped up from his chair as if somehow his rear end had caught fire.

"Martin! What is it?!" shouted Melvin Howard.

I must have looked a wreck with my nose and eyes reddened from my intense allergies and with sweat dripping down my face. He was exasperated, almost to the point of being nervous. But, I was excited so I began proudly:

"I've got a story to tell you."

It was funny almost the way Melvin Howard's face changed from concern to being expressionless to a wide smile, then wider, and finally he chuckled slightly.

"Is that so?" asked Melvin Howard.

"Yeah!"

"Then let's go out to the patio and relax so I can hear this story properly."

Wasting no time, I stepped past him and out onto the patio promptly seating myself upon the end of a chaise lounge. Melvin Howard sat across from me, he too, on the edge of his seat. His eyes focused on me and took in my excitement. He nodded to encourage me to tell my story.

"This really old lady that's real mean on our street always wants me to cut her grass but I never want to so today I told her off because she is always really mean to me." I was talking so fast, and I was pretty sure that my words were getting jumbled but it would have been far worse to miss any of the details. It's hard for people to actually listen to themselves completely when they are speaking; so likewise, I was paying more attention to my thoughts and the course of events I now found reason to tell rather than my delivery. This didn't matter though because I knew I was not a great storyteller like Melvin Howard. Even though my tale was hurried, I was very proud of it, and Melvin Howard appeared to be interested throughout the story's entirety. When I occasionally think back on this particular incident I'm not sure what I was most happy about: standing up to Mrs. McDaniel or finally having an experience that I felt was worthy of sharing with Melvin Howard.

Upon hearing the rest of my story, Melvin Howard reacted as I had hoped he would. He shook his head and chuckled until the chuckle grew into a full laugh that forced his eyes to water. He slapped me on the knee and said, "Nice job, Martin!" I smiled dumbly but gladly like a dog wagging its tail.

"I'll be," Melvin Howard sighed as he reached for his handkerchief. "You know, Martin," he began again. "What did your mother say when you told her this story?"

Now, I was slightly confused. I had never thought to tell her about this incident, not now or ever.

"She will find out, you know?"

For some reason this had not occurred to me. Naturally, Mrs. McDaniel would clue my mother in on my insolent behavior almost immediately after she had regained her wits from my verbal slashing. I suddenly felt trapped. Worry for my own life took over where joy had left off. I felt like I was suffocating. Sweat started to soak my palms. My imagination suddenly showed me another scene from "Cool Hand Luke" where Luke is running for his life because he has just escaped from the work camp. This time the wardens shoot Luke down and he dies never to run again. In my mind it was not Paul Newman, but me, taking the bullet that helped him run his last step.

"Hey, Martin," Melvin Howard had now begun to look consolingly upon me. "Don't worry, yet," he said.

"Okay." I wasn't convinced. My mother would be more than angry.

"Look," said Melvin Howard. "Why be upset about it right now?"

He had a good point since I had all ready done the damage and any confrontation would eventually come anyway.

"The true point is that you stood up for what you believed was right. And Martin, if you really felt you were right then you have to accept your lumps and go on believing. That can't ever be taken away from you." Melvin Howard said evenly.

I tried to relax and still could not even though his voice soothed me.

"Many of the greatest men in the world were soundly punished by others for what they believed to be right. Martin Luther King, Jr., Ghandi, Henry David Thoreau, Jesus, and many others were all punished for their beliefs but never once did they change what they believed just to please all of those who disagreed with them. That principle alone, Martin helps to lend modern man the freedom he has to be a thinker, a builder, a creator, and most of all, a success as a human being."

His philosophy was good and it made me feel better because one thing I was definitely sure about was that Mrs. McDaniel had no right to work me so hard if she was not going to pay me. This I believed and since I believed this; Melvin Howard was right, any punishment delivered by my parents really would not change my attitudes on the subject deep down. So, I listened

71

closely to his words, rehearsing them for my memory. Even though I knew I would never tell my mother my beliefs, I felt my previously discovered confidence welling inside me again. I forced a smile to which Melvin Howard reacted by patting my shoulder firmly and assuring me with a smile that was orchestrated mostly in his crystal clear hazel eyes instead of his face and mouth.

"Maybe I should just tell my mom about it, huh?" I asked.

"Sure. You could do that. But, Martin that is entirely your decision, and I know you will do what is best," he said.

We sat silently for awhile. He looked at me, and I rehashed the circumstances of my run-in with Mrs. McDaniel. I did not feel guilty any more. This was still easily a great personal victory because I had stood up for myself for a change. I was now convinced that I would definitely have to try it again when the opportunity called. After all, I wasn't going to rebel just to rebel. It is usually difficult to tolerate someone who is always standing up for themselves. It was then that I noticed my reflection in the sliding glass door that opened back into Melvin Howard's house. My reflection seemed different, and I thought, 'perhaps I'm getting taller.'

Melvin Howard then broke the silence.

"I remember my second summer over at Mr. Owens' farm." His eyes seemed distant the way they always got when he began to wade through his memories. "I did not like every job that we did there by any stretch of the imagination. At least I did get paid," he continued rubbing his chin that was covered lightly with gray stubble flecked with red.

"What job didn't you like? Mowing the grass?" I asked encouragingly.

"Mowing the grass wasn't bad," he said shaking his head. He wrinkled his brow while he tried to decide which of his responsibilities at Owens' farm he liked least.

"Actually," he said, "mowing the grass was never as bad as picking cucumbers by hand. . . . "

The second week in August had come again just as it had the year before at Harold G. Owens' farm. The "cukes" were ripe, and they had to be picked before the sun dried them all up. The first day of picking, and like the rest of the farm hands, Melvin Howard was trying to put himself in the right frame of mind for the long hours that lay ahead. Actually it was not the long hours that made cucumber season so difficult; but it was the long hours on all fours crawling through the vines in the hot sun. The flies and mosquitoes would bite and the bees might sting the picker who had to ignore everything around him except the "cukes". Missing even one cucumber during picking was considered critical.

The sweat was all ready starting to drip down Melvin's temples. The humidity was high which would only make the temperature keep rising steadily. With one's face down in a bunch of cucumber vines all day, the air would only seem more stifling. Melvin wiped the sweat off of the side of his face with a heavily gloved finger. The gloves were necessary pieces of equipment for the job because the vines were prickly, therefore, subjecting the pickers' hands to a great deal of wear and tear. At the end of each day hand lotion would also become necessary because, despite the thick gloves, a picker's hands and wrists, especially, would become chapped, calloused, and raw.

In addition to the protection needed for their hands, pickers usually wore some padding on their knees. Last summer Melvin Howard was a rookie to "cuke" season and did not wear padding for his knees on the first picking day. The rest of the week was shear hell. After several hours of crawling over the clumpy, rough dirt, Melvin's knees looked like black and blue balloons. The only parts that were not bruised were scratched and raw. This year he would be ready. He thought of how smart he felt because he was prepared for this year's harvest. He knew, however, that no matter how much adequate preparation went into the pre-picking, the work would be grueling, and he was already making plans to hate it. Melvin Howard's lower back started to throb at just the thought of the position he was about to force his body into for nearly the next eight to ten hours.

The first day of picking was always the longest of the week. Last summer, Melvin remembered, the first day of picking was nearly twelve hours. Fortunately, Mr. Owens was not a slave driver so water and short occasional breaks were provided. Last year the "cukes" lasted for a week and a half of solid picking. It was supposedly a very good crop. Somehow Melvin did not recall being impressed.

There would be plenty of others alongside Melvin to assist with the picking because the job involved all twenty of the regular hands plus seven journeymen, and then the majority of the work force would be compiled of migrant workers. The migrant workers arrived two days ago from just outside Fostoria where they had helped another farmer with the picking of his "cukes."

The migrant workers were the hardest working people Melvin had ever met. Work was their life because these people seldom found time for anything else. Since Mr. Owens paid the migrants by the number of bushels they picked, the average migrant would stay in the fields till just after dark every night to only start picking again at just before sunrise. These people seldom took breaks, and the migrants had virtually become immune to the agonies of "cuke" picking. Many of them never wore the knee pads and a few did not even wear gloves. Their hands were weathered and cracked like an old baseball mitt that had been soaked by the rain. The pain from these discomforts, if it was there at all, never seemed to show in the migrants. Instead they always out-picked the regular hands and happily received wages that were considerably less.

Even though Melvin Howard loathed the concept of the existence that migrant workers led, he felt an overwhelming respect for them. Despite their prideless occupations, they were very proud people. It was, he felt, unfortunate that each of them performed the machine-like task of picking vegetables all summer and was never once actually satisfied. Melvin, upon seeing the migrants again this year, decided then that he would never in any way allow his life to be controlled by his work. With a deep sigh to temporarily dispel any other negative accompanying thoughts, Melvin slowly headed for the fields that stretched infinitely before him. He was now nothing more than another cog in the human picking machine that would soon begin its operation.

Traditionally, Harold D. Owens always picked the first "cuke" to begin the annual picking. Every picker would gather in and circle around Mr. Owens to watch him pick the first cucumbers. Mr. Owens had gotten his start in farming through hard work like picking plenty of "cukes" in his lifetime. Through his ceremonial picking of the first cucumbers he tried to make it apparent to every person who worked for him that he was still not above the hard work necessary for success. Picking this first cucumber was far more than a ceremony, however, because Harold D. Owens' hard work oddly enough did not cease there. It was not uncommon to see Mr. Owens picking right along with everyone else. In fact there were times, according to rumor, that Harold D. Owens would try to match the best migrant pickers in the number of bushels picked. As expected, seeing the boss out in the fields also picking cucumbers served as an excellent method of motivation. So, just as they had the year before, the farm hands and migrant workers alike crammed in close to get a glimpse of Harold D. Owens as he picked the first cucumber.

"This year, everybody," began Mr. Owens clapping his hands together. Harvests usually made him very enthusiastic. He once told Melvin that he 'loved harvests because harvests were rewards for hard work.' "This year I'm going to pay everyone double for the number of bushels they bring in."

There was a loud cheer from the throng of pickers.

"So let's get this show on the road and have a fabulous harvest." Harold D. Owens was indeed inspiring and coincidentally Melvin began humming the "Notre Dame Fight Song" in his head.

Then Harold D. Owens knelt down into one of the viney rows, reached into the prickly leaves with glove-protected hands, and snapped off a large green "cuke" coated on one side with dried dirt. He held it up so everyone could see, and he tossed it into the bushel basket of a migrant woman. Also, as in years gone by, Harold D. Owens never placed the first "cuke" in his own basket. Instead, he randomly placed it in another worker's basket which made this little pre-picking tradition fun because it was like playing the lottery. The same person never seemed to get the "cuke" two years straight. Supposedly, the person who was given the ceremonial first "cuke" was granted good luck somehow that would allow them to have a good working day. In Melvin's first year of working on the farm, the first cucumber was given to a journeyman who wound up picking nearly 180 bushels during the first day. Even though many of the workers commented on how "corny" Mr. Owens' plan for motivating his pickers was, deep inside, each of them hoped that they would be the lucky winner of the first cucumber.

"Let's go!!" shouted Harold D. Owens. With that the owner of the farm dropped into the dirt to begin the picking. Unfortunately, the only bright spot in cucumber harvesting was the "corny" tradition. The only possible exception was the paycheck that each worker would receive at the end of the week when the picking would be over for another year.

Melvin like the rest of the workers quickly found a spot and began picking even though he was not really at all eager to begin. The first row or so was not difficult and never was, so Melvin picked quickly. Grabbing hold of the large, dirty cucumber and tossing them into the bushel basket at his side, Melvin had to smile at his efforts as he paused long enough to drag a dusty glove across his dripping brow. The sun was already scorching.

By the first break Melvin had already picked forty bushels full of "cukes". Harold D. Owens, himself had praised him on his efforts so far. Melvin knew that he was on steady pace to pick over two hundred bushels today alone, a pace that was equal to that of some of the best migrants. Melvin was now determined to be the first farm hand to pick more than the migrants. After he had quenched his dust dry throat with some ice water provided by some of the older migrant women, Melvin cut his break short and was soon back on his hands and knees, crawling and picking, making sure that he didn't overlook a single "cuke". The crop had been good again this year.

Melvin finished off two more short rows before he stopped to wipe his brow and to stand so that his knees would not cramp up. So far he felt pretty good, but he knew that that feeling could change at any time. The padding on his knees was definitely making a difference. Last harvest he was wincing after just two hours of crawling between the rows. In addition to the padding, Melvin now had determination. He worked hard and decided to set a goal for himself. He wanted to pick the most "cukes".

When the pickers all broke for lunch Melvin Howard had already picked one hundred twelve bushels, which was slightly off his early morning pace because as he had predicted he would not feel "good" forever. It was not his knees; however, that bothered him, but it was the intense heat. It was only noon and the thermometer by the barn was registering close to ninety-five degrees. Because of the heat, Melvin Howard found himself becoming exhausted easier and more in need of the breaks when they were granted. Nevertheless, the heat had not hindered his performance that much for he was way ahead of is pace from last year and currently found himself in second place by a comfortable margin. Melvin Howard knew this because Harold D. Owens kept a constant count of how many bushels each worker picked throughout the day. Harold D. Owens felt that the friendly competition was great for morale and motivation. The totals at each break time were counted and posted on a board outside of the barn, which gave the whole event the fanfare of a golf tournament. And currently, Melvin was only behind Julio Lopez, a strong, young migrant worker who had come every summer for the last four years to pick cucumbers for Harold D. Owens. Julio, however, was not very far in front of Melvin. He had picked one hundred fourteen bushels. The next nearest competitor to them only had picked one hundred bushels. If the heat didn't affect Melvin or Julio any more than it already had, the competition would fall between them for the day's best.

Melvin felt a great sense of pride upon reading his name near the top of the board. He couldn't wait to tell his father about this achievement for his father always found pride in hard work. Melvin too felt and understood this pride but still he wasn't satisfied. He was close to Julio Lopez. The determination to be the best rose up inside of Melvin again. So before the feeling subsided Melvin Howard cut his lunch short, put on his leather gloves, and headed back to he fields. As he turned to go, he saw Harold D. Owens smile his encouragement. Melvin was inspired. He wanted to run to the fields and start picking in a flurry; however, displaying his zeal like that would be too cocky. Instead, he walked, firm and confident. He had just two bushels to make up to catch Julio, and he was sure that he could do it.

Melvin began picking with both hands quickly. He had a half bushel picked before the migrant workers followed his lead and began picking again. The spiny cucumber vines played hell on his wrists, chafing and scratching them; yet Melvin disregarded the sharp pain even when sweat dripped into the tiny cuts. Melvin's own fast pace proved to be an added inspiration to Julio who was in the row right next to Melvin and picking "cukes" as if he were possessed. The migrants all had a great deal of pride in their own work. Julio Lopez was no different. Not one of Harold D. Owens' regular farm hands had ever beaten any of the migrants when it came to picking cucumbers.

Sweat dripped into Melvin's eyes and stung his vision. He wiped his face off with his right hand while with his left he reached for the next "cuke" on his vine. The sun was hot and the flies were starting to bite, but Melvin thought of nothing else. His mind did not wander to other thoughts for passing the time was not his chief goal. He now moved through the rows with the rhythm of a machine. Next to him was Julio who had now stripped off his sweat-drenched shirt and had tucked it into the back of his work pants. Julio also worked effectively, loading basket after basket. Melvin could hear Julio's heavy panting. It was becoming obvious that the heat would have an effect on both of them. Melvin's head swam for a split second as the field felt particularily humid. He regained his senses when he heard the competitive Julio cough out a heart felt swear word directed toward the bee that had just stung him on the shoulder. It was amazing to see for after the initial pain from the sting, Julio kept right on picking. His vigor was now renewed as if he were angered by the slight setback in which the bee sting had caused him.

It was only then that Melvin allowed himself to think while he picked. While he thought, he watched Julio out of the corner of his eye, trying to study him and trying to understand what gave Julio his drive. Perhaps

Melvin's determination was purely no match for Julio's pride which had allowed the young migrant to know nothing but how to work hard. Melvin still wanted to attain his goal, but he had to wonder whether or not his best would really be good enough to be better than Julio's best. When Julio wasn't picking crops he would be traveling, perhaps sleeping in the back of a pick-up truck along the way until he found himself on another farm settled into another field of "cukes" or maybe tomatoes. Either way, Melvin knew that his own life would change from the monotony of picking "cukes" after the harvest. Julio's life would not change. It was with this attitude that most surprised Melvin about Julio's stamina, for work was his life. For Melvin, the work was simply that—work.

His thoughts cleared and once again centered on the cucumbers, but Melvin could not help but allow himself to be distracted by Julio's efforts.. Breathing heavily, for his energy was being spent quickly by the sun, Melvin snapped the last cuccumber in his row from its vine. He wiped his brow and weakly tossed the "cuke" into a bushel basket beside him. His pores streamed continuously with sweat. He felt exhaustively warm, and he was sure that the sun would continue to bear down on him until he suffocated. Still, out of the corner of his eye, Melvin saw Julio. He had also just finished his row and now was wasting no time getting to the next row. The migrant's efforts were incomparable. Melvin continued to watch Julio and then he huffed out a tired sigh as he got to his feet. His knees were sore after all, but at least, they weren't cut and bruised, just cramped from being in the same position for so long.

After stretching his legs briefly, Melvin tried to start picking again, but the burning enthusiasm he had for the job earlier was now merely but a spark that wavered out more than in. At the next break Melvin glanced at the board by the barn with disappointment in himself for he had only picked one hundred thirty-five bushels. Julio's total now crested at one hundred fifty-two. There would be no hope of catching up to Julio now, especially since the toiling young migrant had waived off this break in order to keep picking. At most, Melvin had toyed with greatness today. At least he had provided an inspiration perhaps to Julio who was able to awaken that pride in him that Melvin knew now far out-shined that of any of the regular farm hands. . . .

"But, Martin, I remember feeling angry that day because I thought that I could have tried harder," Melvin Howard said. "As it was I still finished in the top five overall at the end of the week, but I felt frustrated because I really worked hard, harder than ever. It was just simply that my best wasn't going to be good enough to beat the best migrants."

We both sat in silence for a time and then Melvin Howard stood up.

"Glass of grapefruit juice?" he asked out of the blue.

I hesitated for a moment. "Sure."

I followed him to the kitchen where he reached into a cupboard, pulled out two glass tumblers, and plunked ice from the freezer into each glass as he had done on several of my other visits.

"Martin," he began deliberately. "There are many times that you will do thankless chores in your life. Chalk them up as experience because so often the reward isn't equal to the amount of effort you put in."

He poured the cloudy, yellowish juice over the ice which cracked and popped. "If you work simply for a reward or wages," said Melvin Howard handing me one of the glasses, "you're frequently going to be disappointed." He took a long sip and followed it with a sigh and then a wipe of his moustache.

"Why do I work then?" I asked.

"For the pride of doing a good job."

Quietly we finished our juice then I left for home. By now, I was sure, Mrs. McDaniel had told my mother about my disrespectful behavior. Likewise I now knew I would have some explaining to do for my mother. I also knew that eventually I would end up going back to Mrs. McDaniel's to apologize, not so much to be forgiven, but to appease my mother's worries.

XVII

The rest of the summer for me was basically good. It was also, otherwise, a typical summer for me. As usual my family and I spent several days of vacation in Traverse City, Michigan. It never even bothered me that every summer we vacationed in the same place because Traverse City is beautiful and peaceful. Plus, it was a pleasant change from the humid, sticky weather we were often used to during Northwest Ohio summers. On the vacation, I bought Melvin Howard a post card that had some Indian totem poles pictured on it, which I never actually saw on any of my trips. Regardless, Melvin Howard appreciated my thoughtfulness and the post card remained propped up on his mantle for the remainder of the summer.

Aside from the hot weather there were other things to talk about. Gerald Ford was in the White House and Watergate was finally over. Now, a Democrat from Georgia named Jimmy Carter was America's most popular choice to be president, despite the moans and groans from the die-hard Republicans in my neighborhood. The big story in baseball was very close to home, for the Cincinnati Reds were on their way to repeating as World Series Champions. And, as most kids did then, I had adopted them as "my team." I even bought a Reds ball cap that I wore often to my pride. I wore the hat, but I never swung a baseball bat at all that summer. I was still hung up on my lack of athletic ability.

But, as all good summers do, this one also came to an abrupt end with the start of September. Just as abruptly, I found myself back in a classroom, academically lost and daydreaming. School had not really changed much even though most of the students seemed older or taller. I couldn't help but wonder if any of the other students noticed these latest advancements in maturity in me as I had in them. Some of the boys in my class already had "peach fuzz" on their chins that was actually long enough to shave. My chin had so far refused to sprout hair, which I checked for on a daily basis in the bathroom mirror at home.

The girls in my class were, however, the ones I noticed most. Over the summer many of them had developed from skinny little girls to attractive young women with the emergence of gentle curves where before a frail boney figure had been. I found myself very interested in this latest development of my female classmates. In fact, this current interest of mine often found its way into my daydreams, so that in every one of my imagined adventures I found myself striving for the attention of a particularly shapely leading lady with beautiful, curly hair, big eyes, and a tempting voice that seemed to continually and passionately breathe my name. Occasionally, I would allow the heroines of my daydreams to be played by some of the more attractive girls in my classes. In my dreams, I was the most wonderful person in the world to each one of these girls; yet in reality, they never even noticed me. Socially I did not meet their standards, for I was still very much the same person to them as I was in the seventh grade. Once again, I found myself seated safely outside of the close-knit social circle that many of my classmates had developed. The difference between this school year and others, however, was that my curiosities were now changing, and I was no longer content with my own little corner. It was suddenly important for me to interact with others, especially to gain some type of interest from the opposite sex. The problem was that because I had never really been considered a part of any group, interacting was difficult for me. I needed to learn how to socialize better. After all, gaining the attentions of one girl in particular seemed to be now more important than life itself.

Andria Laurel had moved to my school from a small mining community outside of Pittsburgh, which I knew because the teacher had her explain briefly about herself on her first day of school. But, other than where she was from, I knew very little about Andria Laurel. What I did know was that I found her to be attractive. She had soft, curly brown hair with bright, almost neon, green eyes that seemed to sparkle behind long brown lashes. She smiled often and when she spoke her voice had a hint of an accent similar to that of people from West Virginia. She sat three seats away from me in my math class, so if I was careful I could steal an occasional glance at her while the teacher lectured. She would sit there quietly listening, lashes batting naturally. Her pencil was always poised in her hand. She was a fairly good student. But, the strangest thing about Andria was that I often found myself thinking of her outside of school, and I soon found it difficult not to think about her. Even at Melvin Howard's, amidst his storytelling that previously had been the most captivating thing I had known, I could not put her out of my mind.

One particular day when Melvin Howard and I were trimming some of his hedges he caught me daydreaming. He was busy chopping apart the tops of the hedges to shape them while I stood just holding my trimmers in both hands, staring vacantly at the shrub. In truth, I did not even see the shrub at that moment. I saw instead the brilliant green eyes of Andria Laurel and wished with all my heart that somehow she would notice me as I had been noticing her.

"You know, sometimes that's the whole trouble with this job. You've got to stare these bushes down before you start cutting," quipped Melvin Howard startling me from my daze.

"Oh. What?" Was all I could manage. To avoid the subject of Andria, I started to cut the hedge furiously.

Melvin Howard just coughed, "You all right?"

"Sure. Why?" I returned innocently, but it was quite clear that my mind was not on the work at hand.

"Everything is fine at home?" prodded Melvin Howard.

"Yeah." I was growing impatient because I could see that I would finally confess. Still, I tried to avoid it any way possible. I tried to think of a way to change the topic, but my mind was useless for the moment.

"How about school? Is school okay?" He was persistent.

Now I was sure I would have to tell him because he was getting warmer. I felt suddenly uncomfortable, sweaty, and even a little angry. Despite the nerves, a small part of me wanted to encourage Melvin Howard's interrogation. I was feeling too many things all at once, and none of which I truly understood. I just thought to avoid confronting these confusing emotions I should not commit myself to keeping them secret. At least, that's what I thought I wanted.

"You look like you're preoccupied; like something's on your mind." He would not quit. Every question he asked I was able to dodge up till now. He could see through me. So, I felt very cruel for leading him through this trivial guessing.

I then made a big slip in my efforts to keep quiet.

"Well. . . ," I said shrugging. I was clearly trapped because that single word, 'well' always has an uncanny way of saying that 'there is something wrong' or 'that there is more to the story.'

"Well?" Melvin Howard asked. "What is it?" He had baited the hook successfully which now made my "secret-keeping" measures impossible to uphold.

"At school. . . .," I began slowly as I kept trying to cut the hedges so I could hide my embarrassment. "There's a girl. Her name is Andria."

"Yes?" Melvin Howard encouraged and then he touched my hand firmly so that I would quit cutting the hedge.

Reluctantly I set the trimmers down and continued. "She's in my math class, and I. . .," I shrugged again and took my eyes off Melvin Howard, so I could stare at the ground while I finished.

"And, I think she's sort of cute. I guess."

Melvin Howard smiled slightly and compassionately. Somehow I was sure that he had known all along. I personally felt better after telling him, but my nerves were still on edge. I was chilled with embarrassment, for I had never been able to reveal personal information so confidential before. Now, I was prepared. The questions, I was convinced, were going to come hurtling at me.

We stood quietly for a moment. Melvin Howard smiled but he never asked me anything. Instead, he patted my shoulder and said, "Break time." With this we put the trimmers down beside the hedges and went inside. Even though I was back in school, it was not quite autumn yet and the air conditioning in Melvin Howard's house was great relief from the warm noon-day sun.The two of us walked all the way through the house to the family room where we sat down beside the fireplace. While there was no fire burning, this was the most comfortable place in the house, and no matter what the weather was, the family room held to it a comforting warmth and coziness.

Melvin Howard stretched lazily and turned to me. "How about a glass of juice?"

"Sure, thanks." I was cautious as I watched Melvin Howard cross over to the kitchen and duck into the fridge to get our drinks. I was still on my guard because the questions were sure to start.

"So. . .," began Melvin Howard plunking ice cubes into each glass. The questions were going to start and I became embarrassed for my feelings again. "Have you ever talked to this girl? Andria. Isn't that what you said her name was?"

"Yes, it is Andria." I loved hearing myself say her name. But, I thought that was corny, so I became even more embarrassed.

"Well, what is she like?" asked Melvin Howard happily.

This was a tough question for I didn't know much at all. As a last resort I wanted to make things up just so Melvin Howard would not think that my feelings were a waste of time.

"Well. . .," I paused. "She's cute." I did not have to worry about making things up for I had given it away. "I haven't had a chance to say anything to her yet," I said.

"So, you're admiring this girl from afar." Melvin Howard looked to be thinking hard, almost planning.

"I guess I just don't know what to say to her."

"Well, Martin you're not the only man on the face of the earth who doesn't really know what to say to a woman for the first time." said Melvin Howard shaking his head. "No, that's understandable," he went on. "Men seem like tough customers, but underneath, all men are afraid of rejection, especially from a girl."

"What if I did say something to her?" I asked helplessly.

"Be yourself," commented Melvin Howard. "Because," he continued, "even if she does reject you, you'll know you were honest, and no one can take that from you."

"But, I don't even know where to begin, " I exasperated.

"How about starting with one simple word that has worked for thousands like you," said Melvin Howard confidently. "Say 'hello'."

He made it all sound so easy, and perhaps, it really was.

"I remember meeting my wife, Marcia for the first time," laughed Melvin

Howard as he stretched back in the Lazy-Boy. "I was so nervous." He shook his head and continued to reminisce. "She was so young and beautiful. . ."

XVIII

The campus bustled with activity like every other morning as Melvin rushed to reach class on time as he usually did. This particular morning, however, seemed very different to Melvin. It was a warm day with the fresh morning scents that only early spring can provide, and Melvin took everything in around him as if he were actually seeing them for the first time. Birds chirped playfully in trees and a soothing, light breeze tossed through his hair. While the other students seemed to rush to their various classroom buildings, Melvin felt as if he were floating. The sensation was wonderful. Finally, he came to his own destination. Psychology. He enjoyed the subject and always had; yet today the class was not the reason for his joy. Inside the building the bright fresh sunlight streaked in through high windows up and down the hall, and Melvin thought that he could still hear the birds chirping in his head. He probably would hear them all day long.

"Love is a peculiar thing," thought Melvin Howard. And it was love that he held responsible for his giddiness today. There could be no other reason. Last night he had met the most interesting, most beautiful young woman and today he would see her again. Today he had risen a whole hour before his alarm went off. Not only did he find it impossible to sleep any longer, he could not sufficiently pass the time until he had to leave for class. He tried to study but that was useless. He tried to listen to the radio, but he found it at best a distraction because his mind could do nothing but wander. So, Melvin allowed his mind to wander. It wandered back several hours to the previous evening at the library where he was trying to read an assignment for his history class. The assignment was hard to do, however, because a couple of desks over sat a young woman who was easily better to look at than the black and white printed pages of the history text. Melvin eventually found his gaze fixed on the girl and the book was subsequently forgotten.

She was captivating to him. She was young, probably just a freshman, with short strawberry blond hair that hung about shoulder length. Her eyes seemed to be crystal blue, but Melvin wasn't exactly sure because he had only been able to admire her from a side view. Her body was small and slight. While Melvin watched, she studied intently, seldom looking up for more than just a few moments, at which she then used to take notes. Melvin studied her as if he were magnetized. She had the rare combination that few women attain of wholesomeness and alluring intrigue. It was difficult not to be attracted, and Melvin was simply happy to sit away from her admiring her. He was close enough to be interested without actually being forced to respond to his interest. For now, he was safe to look, for like many guys, Melvin felt somewhat uncomfortable about approaching an unkown woman for the first time. Watching was best for now. He made sure that his admiring the attractive woman was discreet in case she should look up and glance in his direction. So, he tried his best to appear occupied rather than gawking. He tried to struggle back to reading his history. The intention was good, however, his effort was useless. Effective studying was going to be impossible as long as she remained within eyeshot, and Melvin was not compelled to move at all.

Melvin continued to peek over the edge of his textbook watching this nameless beauty until the librarian called out that the library would be closing soon. All around him other students picked up their books and began to head for the doors. Melvin sat dreamily, only half-aware that it was time to go. Finally, the girl stood up from her chair, collected her books, and walked away followed by Melvin's wishful gaze. In seconds she had disappeared from his view, momentarily crushing him emotionally and leaving him frustrated at his own contentment with just watching.

'Once again,' Melvin thought with a disappointed sigh. Once again the interest was there while the courage was not. Trying to meet a woman could many times be like hundreds of fishing stories because it was too easy to tell about the one that got away. Melvin finished picking up his books and headed for the same door she had just stepped through. The librarian then called out that the library was ready to close again to any stragglers who had been too engrossed to either notice or to heed the instructions that it was time to leave.

During the walk back to his dormitory Melvin tried to shake the attractive young student from his mind. There had been other times that his studies were unexpectedly distracted to allow him the necessary time to admire a particular eye-catching beauty. But, no matter how he tried to divert his attention, his attempts were unsuccessful. The more he thought about her the more permanently the vision implanted itself in his memory. Thinking of her made him feel wonderful and tingly, yet he still tortured himself for his cowardice that had prevented him from speaking to her. If he had introduced himself, perhaps he would be talking to her this very moment while he walked her safely to her own dormitory.

Melvin continued walking through the silent night. The campus was always so quiet and solitary. Tonight the campus was also lonely and cold for Melvin Howard who felt the emotional wounds that might lead one to believe that he had turned down his only invitation into heaven.

Feeling sorry for himself, Melvin walked the last several yards to the steps that led to the lobby of the dormitory. Just as he had begun to climb the steps he heard the voice that would change his life from that point forward.

"Oh no!" she exclaimed as the last of the large stack of books she was struggling with tumbled out of her arms and onto the sidewalk.

Instinctively Melvin put his own books down on the steps and went to assist the co-ed who had just dropped her books. "Let me help," said Melvin picking up one of the over-sized manuals. He then knelt to collect some of the girl's other belongings.

"Thank you very much," she replied. Her voice was soft with a touch of a country drawl that aroused Melvin's previously waning interest.

"No trouble at all," said Melvin clutching some of the hand-outs from falling prey to the breeze that always seemed to rise up at night on campus. She had now knelt beside him to pick up some of her own things. Melvin looked at her for the first time since he had offered his help. Before he had only noticed a helpless image; but he now looked at her closely. Simultaneously a smile beamed upon his face for this distressed damsel was the same girl he had been so distracted by all evening at the library. She looked into his face and smiled sweetly, forcing Melvin to look away. He quickly to picked up a notebook in order to avoid staring further into her eyes.

"Thanks again, so much," she said. "You really should not have gone to this much trouble." Her voice was as beautiful as her face thought Melvin. He needed to speak to her now. The odds of seeing her again like this twice in one night would be slim. Her name was a good place to start.

"Melvin Howard's my name. What's yours?" he asked extending his hand. She took his hand and gave it a slight shake. Her skin was so smooth to the touch.

"Nice to meet you, Melvin. My name is Marcia Logan." She smiled through fine open lips that showed a brief glimpse of straight white teeth. Melvin looked directly at her during their introductions and realized that he had been correct in guessing that her eyes were crystalline in their blueness. Melvin Howard got the illusion, despite the darkness all around him, that this delightful young woman before him had the clearest blue eyes he had ever seen. Beyond those eyes, Melvin felt that he could see into a world of compassion, love, and heart; a world that withheld nothing. Melvin was held entranced until she diverted her eyes just enough to dodge his captivated stare. She masked her embarrassment with a giggle.

"You must think I'm very clumsy?"

"Well, it's happened to all of us at one time," shrugged Melvin, trying also to avoid the breathtaking glance that he had just encountered for fear of never being able to look away.

Eventually the two stood and prepared to walk their separate directions, but Melvin realized suddenly that opportunities like this are maybe few. He couldn't stand to let himself allow her to walk away again.

"Where are you headed?" he asked curiously.

"Well, I live just around the corner," replied Marcia.

"Would you mind if I walked with you?" hedged Melvin shyly. "I could help you carry some of these books." He patted the corner of one of the texts in his arms nervously. Then, he noticed that the book was identical to the history book in which he had been unable to read earlier because of her. He was pleasantly surprised by this discovery of common ground and by Marcia's response that followed.

"Sure," she said. "I'd like that, thanks."

Melvin, without hesitation, packed Marcia Logan's books up under his arm and floated beside her to the corner. He was so happy and thankful for the way these events had now transpired that he really didn't remember leaving his own books upon the steps in front of his dormitory.

Melvin and Marcia walked along quietly, stealing glances at each other. Melvin did not feel it necessary to tell her that he had seen her in the library, and that incident did not really seem to matter much any more. Now, he just wanted to think of worthwhile and interesting small talk to make sure he could see her again. His mind, however, was blank and his tongue was speechless.

"It is really nice of you to walk me to my door," said Marcia breaking the silence.

"No trouble," blushed Melvin trying to disguise his growing tongue-tied discomfort. Then he remembered. The history book!

"I noticed that you're taking 201," said Melvin patting the book.

"Excuse me?" She had not understood.

"History," helped Melvin awkwardly.

"Oh yes. One of the many basic requirements I will need to graduate," remarked Marcia with an air of distaste.

"I'm taking the class now myself," said Melvin. The conversation wasn't much but nevertheless it was flowing.

"Really?" asked Marcia. "Do you like it?"

The class was not that bad, but it definitely was not his favorite because he felt that the professor was a bit on the boring side.

"Sure. I suppose so," lied Melvin.

"Well, I'm not too fond of the class myself," said Marcia shaking her head.

"Why not?" asked Melvin. "I mean, it's not my favorite either, but some of it is interesting." The truth really sounded better after all, and he had more to say this way too.

"Who teaches your class because my professor is very boring?"

"Hamler," replied Melvin.

"You don't think he is boring? asked Marcia.

"Sure, everybody thinks he's boring," laughed Melvin. He looked closely at Marcia. She was laughing too, which made him happy. 'She is very beautiful,' thought Melvin. He just could not tire of thinking of that. In addition, Marcia Logan was outspoken, at least, about History 201. Melvin admired women like Marcia who were not afraid to speak their minds and to hold conversations with a man. Too many men, Melvin felt, did not find this trait in today's women admirable. They felt as if the women were trying to take over this "man's world" that everyone supposedly lived in. Melvin, however, found women with Marcia's personality attractive. Liberal women could be more capable of enjoying life. Women like Marcia were apt to find opportunities open for them in this "man's world", and Melvin found the idea of it exciting and worth understanding, not threatening.

"If you would not mind," began Melvin rolling the words over in his head carefully. He was suddenly very aware of his nerves and he did not want to seem presumptuous. "Maybe we could study together?" He said it! He wanted to sigh but that would have been obnoxious and very similar to groveling, so he held his breath to keep it all from escaping rapidly.

"Sure, Melvin. When?"

She had accepted. 'It seemed too easy,' thought Melvin as her quick answer left him a little off-guard. Finally, after smiling and walking for several silent minutes, Melvin acknowledged her acceptance. "Great. Is tomorrow night too soon?" He bit his lip expectantly.

Marcia squinted a moment absently as she thought. "No, that would be fine. Seven?"

"Seven," he confirmed. "I'll pick you up."

"Good." Marcia then stopped in front of some large stone steps that led to her own dormitory. Their first walk was over. Melvin was slightly disappointed. Reluctantly, Melvin handed Marcia's books back to her and awkwardly prepared to say "good night".

"Thanks again, Melvin," said Marcia sincerely, and she extended her hand to him again.

"Welcome," Melvin returned shaking her hand. He could not help but notice in that fleeting moment how soft and dainty her hand was. He stood before her welling with contentment. This had been a good night indeed and he smiled. Marcia smiled back.

"I'll see you tomorrow," she half-whispered. "It was nice meeting you."

"You too," replied Melvin.

With "good nights" spoken, Marcia turned and headed for the door. Quickly she was inside. Now alone, Melvin found it easy to sigh, and he was so glad that he was sure that he was glowing in the dark. He spent a short time in front of her dorm memorizing it and enjoying the thought that Marcia was somewhere inside. There was a chill in the air, but Melvin had not noticed really until now. He turned up his collar and pulled himself away to start the walk home. On the way back to his own dormitory, Melvin hummed a happy nameless tune while his mind rehearsed the course of events that had occurred in the past few hours from when he first noticed Marcia at the library till now when she had accepted his invitation to study with him. The night seemed magical at this point. Tomorrow night would not arrive soon enough for young Melvin Howard.

XIX

Melvin forced himself to take notes while his psychology professor lectured on the theories of psychoanalysis and Sigmund Freud, which was actually very interesting. Still, Melvin was having trouble concentrating on the subject. His mind was clearly not playing an active part in his studies, for he could only focus on the previous evening. He tried to listen, but the only discernible sound was the chirping of the birds echoing in Melvin's head. The information from the professor washed over him like a brook over a smooth rock. Melvin eventually found himself getting lost in the writing of his own notes. The ideas he had managed to transfer from the lecture to paper were jumbled and disorganized. Hopefully, the upcoming mid-term would not be solely on Freud's theories. The test would already be hard enough due to the loss of his books. His books! He just remembered. His books had been missing since last night after he walked Marcia home and up till now he had not been all that concerned. However, now his mind had momentarily quit wandering because the books were a concern—a big one! The books were important not just because of the cost of them, and how without them his classes would be harder, but also he had set up a study date with Marcia. They were going to study history and as Melvin's memory suddenly served, his history text was one of the books he had lost. He had to find that book or else Marcia could possibly think he was just using her to get a passing grade in history. She might lose complete respect for him. He was starting to sweat and panic. 'The date is ruined before it even begins,' thought Melvin helplessly, his mind running wild. He was amazed at himself for not thinking better. He had allowed himself to get so caught up that he had not even realized what a problem losing his books could be.

Psychology seemed to end quickly after Melvin's realization, and he scoffed and stomped out of the building. Where could he begin? He didn't remember exactly what he had done with the books. Crazily, he muttered to himself while he walked back across campus. He wasn't walking in the direction of his next class; instead he was headed home, rehashing the evening before meeting Marcia, searching his memory for clues, but he found none. He continued in this bizarre manner during his entire walk. he forced his brain to think until his temples ached from the stress. He cursed his stupidity under his breath and barely held back the tearing irrational urge he now had for wanting to ransack his room. He tensed his jaw muscles and madly clenched his teeth to stifle the tormented scream that seemed to be building within his throat.

Then just before he exploded, Melvin located a missing piece to the puzzle. Marcia had dropped her own books and he had helped her to recover them. After picking up the books, Melvin had walked Marcia home and had carried her books for her. There was the distinct possibility that Melvin had accidently handed his own books over to Marcia when handing hers back. If Marcia had his books he would surely get them back, however, asking for them might be too humbling since the loss of his books was due solely to his own bumbling carelessness. Looking foolish was the last thing he wanted on his first date with Marcia.

"Damn it," he cursed aloud. There was no other way Melvin Howard finally realized. He would have to call Marcia before their date to see if she had his books. Somehow it seemed that the date had now lost some of its special appeal. For now, reality had hold of him and he was still the same person he was before. He was Melvin Howard, the common kid from Henry County. The ring those words placed in his ears for now was dull and uninspiring. Suddenly, he felt sorry for himself. This would just be another date where he struggled through a pointless conversation about his own past, tried in vain to learn about her, and would spend some hard-earned money on ice cream sodas just so he would never see the girl again. The dream was nice while it had lasted, but for now it was over.

With his expectations now much lower, Melvin stomped slowly up the steps to his dorm. He quietly stepped inside. There were several people sitting in the chairs in the lobby, smoking cigarettes and talking. Melvin recognized nearly all of them as was common at Ohio Northern. Two guys stopped their conversation and waved happy "hellos". Melvin acknowledged them by merely nodding. He did not feel like speaking. Being alone and pitying himself was the only thing Melvin really wanted right now.

Melvin slumped over to the stairs amidst the muttering of others behind him. He had been unsociable, but he also did not care. The lost books and how he had already blown his date were the only things that he could give his attention to for the time being.

"Hey Melvin!" He faintly heard the voice of one of the guys calling his name. Melvin was sure of this so he played ignorant and kept walking.

Just as Melvin Howard began to climb the stairs, a hand, caring and firm, grabbed his arm. Melvin turned and saw the hand also had a face which belonged to his roommate, Paul Cassini.

"Melvin, you okay?" Melvin and Paul seemed to look each other hard in the eyes for a long time.

"Yes, Paul. I'm fine," lied Melvin turning away again.

Paul knew Melvin too well. They were good friends and had been ever since their freshman year. Furthermore, Paul could tell when his friend, Melvin Howard was down.

"All right. Sure?" badgered Paul.

"Yeah, I'm fine," sighed Melvin disgustedly.

Not only had their friendship taught Paul when Melvin was depressed, but it had also taught him not to press the issue. Melvin would come around eventually.

"I'll call you for lunch then."

Melvin nodded again and started upstairs.

Once upstairs and safely inside his room, Melvin locked the door and laid down on the bottom bunk. Even though he was not sleepy, he closed his eyes to shut out all that was real. Maybe by doing this, the sweet dreams from this morning that were conjured by last night would slowly return. He was unable to allow them back so easily. He sat up on his elbows sighing deeply, knowing fully that he was making himself too upset.

Melvin Howard then forced a half smile, and he suddenly felt very silly. Much of his frustration was imagined because the date had not even occurred yet. He was sorry now that he had to Paul too since Paul could have shown Melvin how silly he was being. Paul was good for making light of a situation, and a lighter situation was something Melvin needed.

Melvin slid off the bunk and sat hunched with his elbows resting on his knees, the way athletes rest on the bench. After a few moments Melvin stood up and wandered to the lone window in the room. The drapes were cracked open slightly, allowing a small beam of mid-morning sunlight to shine into the room. Dust from the desk leaped and danced in the sun ray momentarily until it could settle again and again. Melvin sat in his desk chair and looked out the window for what seemed to be a quite a while. During that time Melvin came the closest a man can come to thinking absolutely nothing. His only feelings were summed up in one slowly drawn, quiet sigh that mingled with the dancing dust particles. He would be all right now. His breathing came more relaxed and easy. Involuntarily, he fought the want to laugh tirelessly at himself. Sometimes Melvin Howard felt like this because, like now, there were moments that he thought he was the most ridiculous man around.

Melvin wanted to drag himself from his chair, go back down to the lobby, and tell Paul everything, including a 'thank you' for being concerned. This is what he felt, but he didn't go. Melvin Howard stayed at his desk, gazing out the window, observing nothing, and becoming weary until he finally put his head down, once again shaking up the dust particles.

Melvin awoke about one half hour later to a gentle knocking on the door.

"Melvin? Is it all right if I come in?" It was Paul.

Melvin smiled sleepily and nodded even though the door separated he and his roommate. After another moment and rubbing his eyes, Melvin Howard answered.

"Sure Paul. You have your key?"

Melvin was already unlocking the door from the inside before Paul could respond. Swinging the door open, Melvin found Paul fishing into his pockets, fumbling for his keys.

"You all right, Melvin?" Paul asked without even looking up until he found his key.

Melvin nodded and stepped back so that Paul could step inside the room.

"You're sure? The fellas downstairs didn't think you looked too well."

"I'm fine," said Melvin passively with his gazing once again falling empty out the window. "I'm not too bright, but I'm fine."

"Did you fail a test?" asked Paul, who now leaned against the top bunk.

"No, not really," hedged Melvin. "I just botched up my social life."

"Yeah?"

"Yeah. I met this really wonderful girl walking home from the library last night."

"Okay."

"Well, I talked to her for a little while. She's so cute." Melvin felt some of the magic returning. "I asked her if she would like to study with me and. . ."

"She slapped your face!" Paul interrupted. "Melvin, you seem to always fall for those dames who don't know when a guy is doing them a favor."

Melvin nearly burst out laughing at Paul's inaccurate bluntness. Instead, he just smiled widely to which Paul responded with a cocky, quick chuckle that burst from his throat. Paul's laughing subsided quickly with a shake of his head.

"No, Paul, she didn't slap my face," Melvin chuckled now. "In fact, she really liked me."

"She did?" Paul seemed amazed.

"Yeah, I think," stammered Melvin trying to remain comic and humble.

"She said she'd go?"

"Yes, she said she'd go. Tonight at seven."

Melvin liked thinking this way because it made everything seem special again. The date would, perhaps, turn out just fine.

Then Paul got to the heart of the conversation. "Why are you upset then, Melvin?"

Now, Melvin thought because he wanted to carefully choose his words so that Paul would not think he was silly. There was no easier way, so Melvin tried the honest approach.

"I lost my books."

"So? They'll turn up, right?"

"So?" Melvin glared. Paul shrugged ignorantly.

"The books I lost were the books that I needed tonight for my study date."

"Oh," said Paul slowly and carefully drawing out the word and nodding. He then contorted his face frustratedly as if he were toying with Melvin's dilemma and searching for answers to piece together a good plan. Finally he paused and said, "That could be a problem."

"I know." Melvin knew all too well for he had been over the details of what might happen on his date a million times already. Losing his books was definitely a bad omen. Melvin, by tradition, was not suspicious of "omens", good or bad; but now, he could not be too sure about such beliefs.

Melvin then told the whole story of what happened the night before. He told how he couldn't study because he was so captivated by Marcia's attractiveness. He told Paul about being mad at himself for not speaking to her. He told about helping her with her books, walking her to her dorm, her acceptance of his offer to study together, and everything else that had happened right up to the dreadful moment during his psychology class when he first realized his books were gone. Melvin told everything. Paul listened intently. Melvin searched quietly in Paul's eyes for an answer that could help him. Paul's face held nothing but the consolation that he was concerned for Melvin.

The two sat silent for several moments, Melvin looking down and Paul staring at their image in the full length mirror on an open closet door. Melvin did not move for he was so wrapped up in the many changing signals his emotions were giving out that movement was a far more remedial task. It was Paul, however, popping a cigarette into his mouth, who broke the stillness of the room.

"Well, you want to go get some lunch?"

Melvin just shook his head.

"But. . . ," Paul was just about to lash Melvin with a motherly speech about how 'starving to death wouldn't solve anything,' and he thought better of it. Actually, leaving Melvin be right now was probably best. Paul knew his roommate and knew that Melvin wouldn't let himself waste away over something as trivial as this. For now, Paul would just let Melvin handle this alone. As Melvin's counselor, Paul had done all he could. Melvin had come out of tougher struggles than this one just fine. It was, therefore, safe for Paul to assume that Melvin would also be able to chalk this one up for experience and move on.

"All right, then," remarked Paul. "I'll maybe talk to you in a couple of hours." Paul patted Melvin's shoulder to which Melvin nodded approvingly and mouthed the words, "thank you". Paul then turned for the door to make his exit, however, he stopped suddenly as if he were about to open the wrong door.

"I just remembered something," Paul said and delved into his pockets again. "Ah, here it is!" Paul exclaimed. "This is for you, Melvin."

Melvin held out his hand and took the small piece of folded white paper that Paul handed him. Not only was the paper folded but it was stapled shut with Melvin's name scrawled across the front.

As Melvin unfixed the staple, Paul began, "That weird guy who works at the desk asked me to give it to you."

Melvin knew who Paul meant. Oliver, the desk clerk in the dorm was the recipient of a work-study scholarship that enabled him to go to college cheaper as long as he worked on campus. Many of the other men in the dorm like Paul thought of Oliver as weird because he was slightly effeminate and seemed all too content to work nights in the mens' dorm than to be on a date with a lady. Oliver's queer personality was, however, not of great concern to Melvin now, and upon reading the short note, Melvin might have even been persuaded to declare Oliver as the most wonderful man on earth.

"Fantastic!" he screamed out.

"What?" Paul was quickly and completely confused.

Melvin laughed happily and handed Oliver's note to Paul. Paul looked at the blue-inked handwriting that was even too pretty for that of a woman and read aloud:

"Melvin, your text books were found last night and are waiting at the front desk for you to pick up."

Melvin smiled, slapped his arm around Paul's shoulders, and said, "Paul, I'd love to get some lunch."

XX

"Yes sir, Martin, love can make you do some silly things," said Melvin Howard as he sat back and toyed with his empty glass with his thumb and forefinger.

"Sir?" I pressed.

"Yes?"

"How did the study date go?"

"Wonderful. I picked her up a bit early, so I wouldn't be late and before I escorted her home we stopped off for ice cream sodas."

Melvin Howard seemed captivated by his own memories now. "Marcia looked so pretty that night," continued Melvin Howard. "I recall, she had those pretty strawberry-blond curls donned with a light green ribbon and for some reason that caught my eye."

I listened for now, but secretly I hoped that some day, perhaps, I might be able to enjoy the same type of experience.

"Her eyes were crystal clear and when the streetlights caught them just right they seemed to sparkle like diamonds," breathed Melvin Howard happily.

"That night," he went on, "we were able to talk about anything. We had so much in common, and I felt so comfortable talking to Marcia that I was certain right then that I had stumbled into something very special."

I was worried slightly by what he had just said because Melvin Howard had said that 'he knew he had stumbled into something very special.' How had he known? Little did I know, at the time, the question that tossed about in my head was probably as old as time itself, and the answer to this infinite question still remains a mystery. The peculiar thing to me was that love basically played to no set rules; which to me seemed to make it that much more difficult to understand.

"We even managed to study a little too," chuckled Melvin Howard.

"What then?" I asked innocently.

"Well, I asked her if I could call on her again soon. She said, 'sure'."

Melvin Howard smiled broadly, glowing as if the incident of kindling the romance between he and Marcia was happening all over again.

"How did you know, sir that you should ask her out again?" I implored even though I was afraid of getting too personal.

"She kissed my cheek as we said good night," smiled Melvin Howard.

'That would do it,' I thought. If Andria kissed my cheek, not only would I call on her again I would probably fly to the moon under my own power, as well as do absolutely anything for her.

"But, Martin," Melvin Howard added, "the moment I knew that I should not let this girl get away without at least another date didn't really occur when she kissed me."

"When did it?" I asked.

"When I decided to tell her all about my day leading up to the date."

I wrinkled up my forehead. He had lost me.

"I told her the whole humorous story about losing my books and literally losing my mind over it."

"Didn't she laugh?" I asked confusedly.

"Yes, she did. We both did. We roared with laughter." Melvin Howard sat back and paused, enjoying this memory to its fullest. "Because Marcia made me feel so comfortable, I could truly be myself, and therefore, I could laugh at my own silliness. That, Martin, is I've decided, a rare attribute in a woman."

"How come?"

"Well, son, I'm not going to shun your questioning by saying that you'll find out someday. Instead, I'll tell you: If you find a woman that allows you to be yourself and she still likes you in spite of that, hold on to her. Chances are, she's one in a million. When you discover that one woman, Martin, love really isn't very difficult to find at all."

I smiled back at him to thank him for the advice. Even though I still did not know how it was that Melvin Howard had found what he was looking for in Marcia, I was grateful for the fact that he did not just leave me groping by saying: 'You'll find out some day' like so many others might have. I even felt like I had some of my sorts about me once more after Melvin Howard's story. The reason for this was as unsure to me as the comprehension of my feelings for Andria and my instincts that might trigger when I actually would be in love. It was true because, despite the fact, that suddenly everything, including my own feelings, seemed so foreign, I felt comfortable and not as ill-prepared as I had previously imagined. After all, I could say "hi". I would be nervous, but Melvin Howard had said that that would be all right since everyone feels that way at first.

I wanted to thank him for his compassion, and was about to when I noticed a different look on Melvin Howard's face. While I paused our conversation long enough to sort through my own feelings on love, Melvin Howard's memories had apparently taken him elsewhere. He now seemed downcast compared to his previous reminiscent joy. He now appeared sad, and the expression his face held, while it was generally uncharacteristic of him, was not entirely strange to me. I had seen him in this state once before when we had discovered the photograph of his daughter, Janie while cleaning up the basement.

Without warning, my discomfort returned in a different vein. Now, this discomfort posed as helplessness instead of adolescent confusion. I didn't know how I should react. Perhaps I should have asked if he were all right to encourage him to talk and then maybe this seemingly grief-stricken memory could be exposed and once again beaten back by the strong-willed Melvin Howard that I had come to respect and recognize as my only true friend.

Before either of us could speak, Melvin Howard stood up and crossed over to the mantle above the fireplace, which waited silently for winter to begin. The fireplace would have to wait, however, despite the frosty and depressing story that was about to slowly melt off of Melvin Howard's memory.

"My wife," Melvin Howard began, eyes welling with tears, "died in her sleep about five years ago, and for me, the memory is still too fresh." Melvin Howard breathed heavily and uneasily, for once appearing very old. For me, after hearing the opening words to the story that was soon to follow, the realization that there is no skillful nor gentle way to tell a story about death came rudely back.

XXI

Early spring is a peculiar time in Northwest Ohio, for the weather is so unpredictable. It had been a typical March day. The wind had blown cold, even freezing at times, and the icy rain had fallen most of the day despite the weatherman's forecast of sunny skies and temperatures in the low fifties. Regardless of the unpredictability of the weather, life in Northwest Ohio carries on and the inconsistent weather just gives everyone more to complain about. As this typical March day advanced into evening, Melvin Howard found himself kicked leisurely back in his La-Z-Boy recliner reading The Blade with little interest while he focused at least half of his attention on the news. The reporter was giving updates about the war in Viet Nam. Maybe there would be some report of his son's long-awaited return from the hell he must be enduring in those God forsaken jungles. Eventually Melvin Howard focused solely on the television until he was convinced that a surrender was still not at hand.

'War was a ghastly thing,' thought Melvin Howard flipping back to the sports. UCLA seemed like they were once again the team to beat in basketball, according to the article Melvin was reading about the team's latest victory, a key one to push them into the tournament quarterfinals.

Melvin shook his head in amazement after skimming through the UCLA article. John Wooden certainly knew basketball. Then, Melvin chuckled slightly. If John Wooden really were a "wizard" as all of the papers called him maybe Channel 13 should hire him to do the weather.

Finally Melvin got completely bored with the newspaper, folded it up, and placed it on the floor beside his chair. He started to lie back in the recliner, thinking that a nap might feel good; however, Melvin then thought better of it. Instead, he checked the clock above the mantle for the time. It was nearly seven o'clock and Marcia, his wife, would be home shortly. She had gone out to a friend's home for a "Tupperware" party. It seemed harmless as long as she didn't buy anything, which Marcia had agreed on as well. It wasn't the "Tupperware" that drew Marcia Howard out of her home that evening, but simply, the social contact of getting together with her friends. While Marcia herself wasn't a gossip, she loved to hear all the latest news of the neighborhood from the other girls. She always described it as "entertainment." This always reminded Melvin of reading the National Enquirer or some other gossip page at supermarket check out lines. Those papers were so unbelievable, and while Melvin had never actually bought one before, he found them certainly entertaining to glance at while waiting in line with a cart load of groceries.

Melvin always considered Marcia's nights with the girls to be a necessary strength in their relationship as husband and wife. After all, he had his occasional poker nights, football games on Sunday afternoons, and his weekly Jaycees meetings. With both of them enjoying lives outside of their marriage as well, it was easier to understand why being together was so pleasurable. Because of this sound philosophy, Melvin and Marcia Howard had managed to not only stay married for nearly thirty-four years, but they also managed to stay happy. The number of years even staggered Melvin when he actually thought about them and the many experiences he and Marcia had shared. Through their marriage they had managed to both graduate from Ohio Northern University. Both of them, while currently retired and loving it, had been successful professionals in their fields; he in insurance and she in bank management. Fortunately, they were able to put some money aside, here and there to buy the beautiful home in which they now lived. The years had seen Melvin and Marcia raise two fabulous children. Thomas, their son was currently fighting in Viet Nam for a cause that was not clear cut, but to go was the young man's choice. For that powerful decision, Melvin Howard greatly respected Thomas and perhaps even envied him slightly. All the respect in the world, however, would not bring his boy back soon enough. For this, Melvin and Marcia had shared tears, hugs, and fearful dreams. These feelings of fear over losing Thomas were justified for the Howards because their youngest, their little girl, Janie died tragically when she was sixteen in a car accident on the night of her prom. Together somehow, Melvin and Marcia had managed to live past the horror of Janie's death and had, gradually through time, chosen refuge in the beautiful memories of Janie from when she was living.

For Melvin and Marcia the bad times had truly been bad, but still these were far outshadowed by the good. Being with Thomas for his first haircut when the youngster was three always brought a smile to Melvin's face. There was a picture of this "great family moment" in the photo album, but to Melvin Howard the memory alone seemed just as vivid. He remembered how Thomas had been so good. The little boy sat up in the big barber's chair so proudly, never flinching once as the barber wielded the razor and the scissors all around the boy's head. Thomas had been brave, indeed, and posed a toothy little grin when Marcia had aimed the camera at him perched proudly in the chair and on a soft pile of his own hair. From that particular moment forth, Melvin should have realized his son would go on to be a soldier. Melvin wanted to laugh out loud because until now he had failed to see the possible connection between his son's first haircut and his son's volunteering for military service.

With Janie, Melvin and Marcia had had plenty of wonderful moments. The time in particular that suddenly crept into Melvin's wandering mind was the time that Janie had joined the 4-H Club when she was ten. Melvin and Marcia agreed to their daughter's joining of the organization one night after Janie talked on and on, enthusiastically about how her best friend Sharon McGuthrie had joined 4-H. Indeed, the possibilities that could come from Janie's involvement with 4-H seemed only positive, so the Howards decided that the organization would be a profitable experience for an outgoing youngster like their daughter. Janie was ecstatic over her parents' decision, and as Melvin recalled, "could not thank them enough". He smiled contently, remembering the vigor with which young Janie had leaped up into his arms to thank him with a hug. It was easy, from that point forward, for Melvin Howard to understand why a man's daughter was the best possible encouragement for his own ego. To young Janie Howard her father was "the greatest man in the world." By making the decision to let her join 4-H, Janie's attitude about her father was far from changing. Melvin and Marcia Howard had been correct in thinking that the involvement in 4-H would be positive for Janie because through the four years in which she participated in the organization she was always energetic and hardworking. For her efforts, Janie won several awards through the years for the various 4-H projects that she had pursued. Melvin remembered, however, that it was after Janie's initial meeting with the club that he had any second thoughts about his decision. His daughter came home that evening after her first meeting and happily announced that she had loved the meeting and had already made a decision about her project that she wanted to do for the county fair. Melvin and Marcia were proud of their daughter's enthusiasm, so with nods and smiles they encouraged her. It was then that Janie said that she wanted to raise "bunnies", specifically, "big white bunnies."

The truly comical part of this memory was that after some private discussion between he and his wife away from Janie and some more discussion on the subject with his daughter, Melvin reluctantly consented and helped Janie build three rabbit pens in the backyard next to the garage under the circumstances that Janie, and Janie alone, would see that the rabbits got proper care. Because daughters are wonderful for a father's ego, fathers will often find themselves frequently giving in to their daughters' wishes. What Melvin Howard had wrongly prepared himself for though was that he would be taking care of Janie's rabbits by himself, despite the initial agreement between he and his daughter. It was here, at age ten, that Janie really proved to both Melvin and Marcia that she was a special person. Not only did she readily accept the responsibility of taking care of the rabbits, she studied her hobby as if it were a science. She was also careful so that her hobby did not multiply, a mild fear of her parents. That summer at the county fair, in fact, Janie's "big white bunnies" won a blue ribbon. Every summer after that, Melvin and Marcia were eager to try to help Janie with her projects, and she never refused their assistance nor did she work any less. Because of this, Janie's "bunnies" were consistent champions, and Melvin and Marcia retained many fond moments in their memories of being close to Janie while she grew up through the tough early years of adolescence.

As Melvin reclined in these memories, he had completely forgotten that he had been bored just minutes ago. He could not wait for Marcia to return now, especially so he could ask her if she had ever thought of the connection between Thomas getting his first haircut and him going to the army. She would enjoy that and probably see the connection that he had also seen, and together again, they could forget how afraid they were for their brave son.

Marcia usually arrived around twenty minutes after the time she told Melvin that she would be getting home. Melvin had grown to accept this as one of Marcia's idiosyncrasies, and even though, he did not like her loose understanding of time he also knew that twenty minutes was not something to be angry about. When they were younger they did have an occasional spat because younger couples, it seems, spend several years still getting used to one another's habits. Melvin and Marcia had, after all, finally realized that the efforts they went to to change each other were basically pointless. Melvin knew that even to this day Marcia got irritated about the fact that he never seemed to squeeze the toothpaste tube at the bottom, working up. Instead, Melvin had somehow acquired the very wasteful habit of squeezing the tube in the center, leaving the tubes crumbled and twisted and apparently empty before their time. Then, as every man has probably been confronted with at one time, Melvin Howard was also accused of leaving the toilet seat up. Despite the inconveniences this presented to the female members of the house, Melvin could never remember to put the seat down. All in all, Marcia's tardiness and his own undesirable squeezing of the toothpaste and absent-mindedness concerning the toilet seat seemed to matter very little in light of what he and his wife had built together. No matter how he squeezed the toothpaste tube Marcia had vowed nearly thirty-four years ago to love him, and despite Marcia's lateness, Melvin had made the same commitment to love her. And he did. Because of these commitments and emotions it would take more than idiosyncrasies to come between Melvin and Marcia.

Tonight was no different than others in which Marcia was out, for at roughly 7:20 or so Melvin sat up quickly to the sound of the heavy wooden front door clunking out of its jam and then opening as Marcia gave it another push. With the door out of the way, Marcia stepped in toting an over-stuffed purse and a small brown sack that rattled muffled sounds. This was not good. However, Melvin laughed the contents of the brown sack off as one of those idiosyncrasies that weren't worth worrying about, because no matter how many times Marcia had promised her husband that she would not buy anything, Melvin knew that she would come back with at least one item. The item would not be entirely useless, but yet, it would not really get nearly enough use to be termed "useful."

"Hello, Dear," smiled Marcia and then her shoulders shook involuntarily as one last chill from the cold dampness outside went through her.

"Hi." Melvin stood up from his chair and stepped over to her and kissed her cheek. She blushed slightly and hugged his neck. After their embrace, Melvin helped his wife off with her coat.

"I'm so sorry that I'm late, Melvin," apologized Marcia sincerely.

"That's okay," returned Melvin. "I was only a little concerned because of the nasty weather."

"Well, don't worry. As you can well see, Dear, I'm home now," consoled Marcia patting her husband's shoulder.

Marcia still had the little brown bag in her hand and started walking through to the kitchen with it. Melvin followed inquisitively. He really didn't need to be so nosey because Marcia always showed him what she bought even if she knew that he would hate it. No matter how much he hated what his wife had bought, Melvin, somehow through the years, was always discrete in his negative opinions. This was important because sometimes she bought him presents that he didn't always want. Still, he never wanted Marcia to think that he did not appreciate her thoughtfulness. That was what was really important here; not the presents, but the thoughtfulness to just say "I care". Melvin always tried to do the same for her whenever he went some place without her, and some of the things Melvin Howard brought to his wife were, in effect, useless except for the one overshadowing fact that "whatever it was" symbolized his caring for her.

"I know what we agreed on about not buying anything," started Marcia. "But, they had some really cute salt and pepper shakers," Marcia said lowering her head and curling her lip like a child caught snitching cookies. This little pout of hers was always part of the conversation, and it usually worked with Melvin.

"Let's see them." Melvin acted enthusiastic over the damn Tupperware even though he wanted to laugh at his wife's behavior as well as his own. Really Melvin could care less about the Tupperware, but he knew Marcia would struggle through a few more rationalizations which were always cute to see. Before she began, Marcia Howard unveiled the salt and pepper shakers. The tiny molded pieces of Tupperware were fashioned into the shapes of Mickey and Minnie Mouse; and while these two characters as cartoons are cute, as salt and pepper shakers, they were exceptionally tacky. Melvin could not help but laugh a little, and he took Mickey from Marcia's hand for a closer, more personal look at which he laughed even louder. 'These are simply hilarious,' thought Melvin quietly.

"Well, you know how much we both love the Disney characters," stammered Marcia who now felt it necessary to defend herself as well as the salt and pepper shakers. "I just thought that they would be something fun to have around. Sort of like a keepsake or a collector's item."

Melvin still smiled at the ridiculous pieces of tableware. 'It was astounding

103

how tacky they were,' again thought Melvin. Then the thought of the two fun-loving mice situated on his breakfast table and he actually picking up Mickey to lightly pepper his eggs on a Sunday morning for some reason forced a loud hoarse laugh out of Melvin. "So much for discretion," said Melvin aloud choking back his sudden burst of laughter until he coughed.

"They are really pretty tacky aren't they?" remarked Marcia taking the smiling Mickey back from her husband.

Both of them laughed a little then, and Melvin hugged his wife closely and kissed her on top of the head. She responded to his affection by snuggling closer and then she said, "Melvin, the biggest reason I chose those tacky little things was because I was thinking about you." Now Melvin was confused because he did not really understand what she was driving at. He even felt a touch guilty for behaving the way he had moments ago.

"Remember when we first started dating?" pressed Marcia sentimentally.

"Yes?"

"Well, remember when you took me uptown to see the movie, "Fantasia"?"

"I guess so, sure."

"That was the first film we ever saw together," said Marcia. "And there was a Mickey Mouse cartoon short before it." Marcia smiled up at Melvin brightly, and he smiled back. He did feel slightly guilty after all even though that had not been Marcia's ploy. She was sincere. Melvin knew her too well by now to think otherwise.

"I love you, Marcia," responded Melvin honestly.

"I love you too," said Marcia and she hugged Melvin closer.

'There it was again,' thought Melvin as he held tightly to Marcia, the "thoughtfulness" that always seemed so important.

The rest of the evening passed as usual. Melvin re-read the paper until he got bored, and Marcia cross-stitched, often becoming entranced in the television set that hummed lowly for background noise. Neither Melvin or Marcia ever enjoyed complete silence but with the television or some music playing these quiet evenings at home were content and pleasant. Eventually, Melvin's boredom with the newspaper led him from his chair and into the kitchen for a bowl of ice cream. No matter what the weather, ever since he had retired, Melvin Howard ritualistically raided the freezer nightly for a bowl of ice cream. It wasn't so much that he loved ice cream; but rather, he found eating ice cream to be relaxing because it was difficult to eat ice cream quickly without it driving a sharp spike of coldness through his forehead. So, Melvin didn't even risk the discomfort. He took his time, savoring each creamy bit, sucking on the spoon for a time, and finally finishing as Ed McMahon introduced Johnny Carson.

"Do you want some ice cream, dear?" asked Melvin over his shoulder as he padded to the kitchen. "Vanilla fudge," he added.

"No thank you," returned Marcia who was currently wrapped up in the television again.

Marcia never wanted any ice cream, yet Melvin always asked her every night. She never got edgy about his asking either.

Melvin returned to the living room with a dish of ice cream, spooning into it before he even sat down again in his chair. Melvin sat down finally and smiled at Marcia as he rolled a huge delicious bite around in his mouth. She smiled back at him and reached her hand out to touch his arm. After a time of this smiling and almost telepathic conversation that held them transfixed to one another's emotions during these quiet times of the evenings the late news came on. Now, the couple's emotion changed from passive, contented warmth to grave, desperate severity. Viet Nam would be on television again tonight, for it always was. Their son was there.

Both Marcia and Melvin had paused their activities, Marcia with her cross-stitching and Melvin with his ice cream, so that they could more easily concentrate on the latest reports from Saigon. Every night at eleven o'clock Marcia and Melvin joined one another to listen intently to the news in their own silence. They had held these private hopeful vigils every night since Thomas' departure for the god forsaken war. Every night there was never any news about Thomas or his company; but Melvin felt that definitely no news would be good news. So as long as there was no news indicating that something terrible had happened to Thomas, as had happened to so many other young soldiers, Melvin Howard would positively assume that his son was still alive and was not a prisoner of the Viet Cong.

"I wish Nixon's kids could go fight over there," said Melvin cold and stern.

"That might certainly speed things up a bit," thought Marcia aloud, eyes still glued to the death flickering set.

Melvin was tired of blood on his TV, and it appeared that the war might never actually end. The only people that really seemed to want this political bloodbath to end were completely powerless in the final decision needed to end it.

"Things never seem to matter as long as it's happening to somebody else's kids," sighed Melvin. "When it's your own then you tend to see the light."

It was true. Since Janie's death neither Melvin or Marcia had taken a drink of alcohol, nor had they driven without a safety belt. The issue of drinking and driving had never been a very serious concern to the Howards until it had personally affected their family. The war in Viet Nam had given Melvin a very bad feeling at its outbreak, but the significance of President Johnson's supposed "police action" did not truly gain Melvin's concern until his own son became involved. Somehow Melvin Howard could not help but feel a little depressed again at the thought of Thomas actually volunteering for combat.

Melvin felt some moral regret for wishing the same trauma on Nixon's kids because, despite the fact that the President could be moving faster to end the war effort, he knew Mr. Nixon was only doing the best he could with what Johnson had left behind. Perhaps more pressure was needed by the American public to get the President to pull the troops out of Viet Nam, yet Melvin knew that he did not want Nixon's job—ever.

105

Eventually, the horror and depression of the war and the news in general ended for another day, seguing into a commercial break. Melvin could not help but think how depressed the society of which he was a part had become. There was seldom a hint of "good news" any more. It seemed that only the cold, horrible facts and disastrous events were the only news items that the public was interested in today. With this, Melvin reached over and took his wife's hand and squeezed it tight. She responded with a consoling smile. Things would be all right.

Melvin returned to his ice cream, which had started to melt a little, and Marcia began cross-stitching again. She was making a covering for a jewelry box that she had bought for her sister. Melvin was usually impressed by the results of Marcia's finished products, however, to him cross-stitching seemed tedious and not at all relaxing.

Soon the commercials stopped and Ed McMahon came out and introduced Johnny Carson, who gave the traditional nightly monologue. Tonight Johnny's act was only mildly funny to Melvin. Still, the audience cheered and laughed any way. 'Life definitely goes on,' thought Melvin whose mind was still with Thomas somewhere in the jungles far away from Northwest Ohio.

Midway through the "Tonight's Show" Marcia put down her cross-stitching project and stretched. "I'm tired," she yawned. "I think I'm going to bed. You?"

"I'll be up in just a bit," said Melvin not straying from the television until Johnny cut away to another commercial, and then Melvin looked up at his wife. She looked to be exhausted, and she yawned again before she turned toward the stairs. She was still a beautiful woman, and always had been. Then like an innocent school girl Marcia turned to her husband, smiled sleepily, and blew a kiss to him. At this Melvin laughed slightly and held his right hand up to pretend like he actually caught the kiss. He watched her continue up the stairs. Being married to Marcia was never dull and never difficult. She did not nag him at all like he had heard some wives do to their husbands. She enjoyed cooking and wasn't interested in equality, even though Melvin always treated her equally. She accepted his faults and seemed to understand his moods. Most importantly, the two of them enjoyed spending time together.

Melvin returned from his thoughts to see the final credits of the "Tonight's Show" rolling on the screen. With this he reached forward and shut off the set and flicked off the light. Melvin then fumbled briefly in the darkness of his own living room for several moments until he re-discovered his own staircase and started his climb, feeling each step with his toe cautiously before actually stepping. Once at the top of the stairs, Melvin slowly worked his way down the hallway to the bathroom. It was here that he finally clicked on a light because through his many years of marriage to Marcia he had learned that she generally fell asleep quickly, especially when she was tired; so he wanted to avoid the possibility of waking her, if she was indeed already sleeping, by turning on the hall light that might shine brightly underneath their bedroom door. Deep down, Melvin had probably believed at one time that the hall light was not really bothersome at all to Marcia; but stumbling down the hall in the dark had become habit to him. Even though Marcia had never issued a demand to Melvin about the hall light, he practiced this ritual nightly, as if in another silent way he were saying, "I care about you." Once again, to himself, Melvin decided that this is what made his marriage to Marcia a success.

With the light in the bathroom on Melvin squinted until his eyes could re-adjust to their temporary suspension from light and then shut the door so that none of the light's brightness would leak out into the hallway. Alone with the light, Melvin picked up his toothbrush, applied a glob of Crest to its bristles, and began brushing carefully his gums as well as his teeth. Melvin still had all of his teeth, a physical feat for which he was very proud because several of his friends had already lost most of theirs to the worst type of tooth decay—old age.

After his nightly bathroom routine, Melvin stepped out of the previously lighted bathroom to the now dark hallway again. Quietly, trying to dodge the parts of the floor that creaked the most, Melvin finally made it to the bedroom and carefully eased himself beneath the covers, sliding in beside his wife who was already resting comfortably. Her back was to him, yet he watched her sleep. Her breaths came slowly and effortlessly. Each night Melvin usually watched Marcia sleep; it was a practice he had been doing for thirty-four years. Maybe he was still, even after all these years, amazed by her presence there, or perhaps, she was symbolic of his own peace. The answer for his behavior was never exactly clear. That is, if there even was an answer. Just like all other nights before this one, Melvin watched as Marcia lay quietly under the blankets sighing the sweet, relaxing melody of sleep. Sleep, it seemed, brought the childish side of Marcia out, for she still curled herself up into a semi-fetal position despite being already a couple years into her retirement. Eventually, Marcia's contentment with sleep would become contagious and Melvin too would drift off quietly to celebrate the rapturous comfort of slumber with his wife.

As he watched, Melvin could feel his own eyelids starting their descent. Before long he would be resting as well, but for now, he remained slightly awake, peacefully watching his wife's breathing. He never told Marcia about this routine of his though. This routine was something that he kept to himself because he felt that perhaps she might have at some point in their relationship become embarrassed by his quiet, nightly observations. His glance, however, was one of appreciation—for Marcia and for himself. Even if Marcia was fully able to understand Melvin's necessity for this nightly behavior, any future observations would be unnatural and not as satisfying to him. So, Melvin never told her. These moments were important to him and talking about these moments would only change them forever in his mind.

Finally, Melvin's brain ceased conscious thought for another day; for as determined by other nights like this one, Melvin Howard's eyes closed tightly, shutting out light and filling his mind with vivid dreams while his body was slowly quenched of its need for slumber. Beside him, Marcia Howard coughed hard and loud just one time, raised her hand to her right temple that suddenly pumped with pain, and then threw her head back slowly onto the pillow again; this time wincing a little before she was able to doze off. Even death can be stealthy and quiet in its duty of claiming the living.

"That morning when I woke up, Martin," gulped Melvin Howard fighting back the tears that probably fell every time he recalled this memory, "Marcia was lying very still beside me. She looked the same as she had when she had been sleeping. Peaceful and quiet." He shook his head as if to deny the memory entrance into his mind again. It was at that moment that the tears began to slowly trickle down Melvin Howard's cheeks. They did not come in a flood, but instead these tears fell slowly and painfully, as if it even hurt him too much to cry.

"I'm sorry," he apologized wiping his eyes with a dingy white handkerchief that he kept balled up in his back pants pocket. "It's been a few years, but I still feel her loss immensely," breathed Melvin Howard blowing his nose between words.

I did not respond out of youth and ignorance and somehow I knew that I didn't really have to respond either. Melvin Howard was not only a man of great character but he was also a man of great feeling. As he had taught me through these months of friendship, I knew that any great man should not be sorry about showing his true feelings. I also knew that by speaking I could only ask more questions, which might be more difficult for him. So, I stayed quiet and listening. When his eyes re-filled with tears I desperately fought to keep my own tears from surfacing. I fought this wish to cry so hard that my throat bobbed as if I were unable to swallow. But, Melvin Howard was not afraid to cry, for at that moment, the emotional dam controlling his tears burst. His shoulders shook and he buried his face in his hands, occasionally wheezing and coughing when the crying had made it impossible for him to breathe properly. From this display I tried to turn away for fear of disturbing him more, but I found my efforts were useless. Strangely, I felt as if my being there was actually lending a form of support to him; but the answer to this I never found out for sure. I stayed, and Melvin Howard's sobs deepened and eventually lessened until he was merely wiping his eyes and sniffing to catch any of the remaining tears trying to escape.

At that point in my life I had never seen an adult man cry so heavily; but also at that point in my life, I was still learning how fine the line between childhood and adulthood can sometimes be.

Melvin Howard eventually stopped his crying all together and gave his nose one last blow as if to punctuate the end of this momentary return to grief.

Once again, I recalled the time Melvin Howard had told me about Janie's death and how I remembered being incapable of truly relating to his feelings. This similar feeling of inadequacy again welled inside of me. Death, so far, had not claimed a large role in my life as it had in Melvin Howard's. Justifiably, his predicament was alien to me and in efforts to understand more clearly, my eyes fixed solidly on him while my mind became entranced. I felt like I was staring but I could not stop myself. Then Melvin Howard looked up. His eyes met mine until I blushed and turned away. "Martin, I'm so sorry." He forced a raspy chuckle and sniffed into his handkerchief again. "I should plan my outbursts a little better so that I'm not entertaining guests when I have them. "

"No, sir. Really, that's all right," I offered as the only bit of consolation I could muster.

"Well, you will have to forgive me because like I said I am still very sensitive where Marcia is concerned."

I just nodded. This I could understand completely, and I felt his grief whisk through me like a cold breeze off Lake Erie.

"The damnedest thing about it all, Martin is the way it all happened." Melvin Howard shook his head again. His eyes then seemed to glue themselves to a particular spot on the floor. "The doctors who examined her decided that the cause of death was due to an aneurysm in her brain. Apparently, they told me, one of her blood vessels swelled and finally burst under the pressure," he sighed deeply. "Supposedly, she died instantly without much pain." Then he just stared at me long and hard. "As if that is supposed to make me feel any less," he breathed.

"The only thing I can figure," said Melvin Howard hopefully, his eyes turned toward the ceiling, "is that God got a little jealous, so he called one of his angels back to join him." With eyes still fixed on the ceiling, or even beyond, Melvin Howard forced a radiant smile of his own that was not, unfortunately, bright enough to distract me from noticing one more tear slowly slide down his cheekbone.

I decided then that regardless of what "forever" really meant, physical love could never survive. With my heart reaching out for Melvin Howard in his woe, my eyes quite possibly saw him pledge his spiritual love to Marcia and her memory, a bond that was definitely undying and timeless.

XXII

Soon the last few warm days of fall turned dismal and cloudy as only Northwest Ohio can with winter on the way. The days were colder and shorter now, which made very little work for me at Melvin Howard's house. Nevertheless, he occasionally had some chore for me to accomplish and if he didn't we would spend the time in his family room talking about how school was going for me, or sometimes he would even tell me a story, as he was so prone to do.

Melvin Howard paid me my wages just the same whether I worked or if we spent the day inside talking and drinking grapefruit juice or hot chocolate. Sometimes I felt guilty because of his generosity and would insist that he did not have to pay me. But, he insisted that I take the money.

"If I'm fool enough to give you money Martin, could you please be fool enough to take it?" he would say waving two tens and a five before me until I could no longer resist the temptation.

Melvin Howard's reasons for giving me the money were justified to him because he felt that if I was going to come all the way over to his house expecting to work that I deserved payment. This I appreciated, but I also knew that it was Melvin Howard's company that I treasured most—not his money. Besides, Melvin Howard always wondered if he were keeping me from my friends, and I never could get the courage up to tell him the truth. He was my only friend. Nearly a month had passed since I had confessed my attraction for Andria, and I had just recently found the nerve to say "hi". With her, Melvin Howard had been right; for once I had crossed the first barrier of meeting Andria, it seemed much less awkward to be around her. I even engaged myself in casual conversations with her, but I was still hesitant to pursue things further. While my confidence was definitely growing, it was still not stable enough to help me stand on my own socially.

Perhaps Melvin Howard knew that he really was not keeping me from any other friends; but if he did, he never showed it. With him I was always comfortable and out-going, for it was here that my confidence seemed to be in training. Melvin Howard encouraged me in everything and made all these things he spoke of seem possible for me if I displayed the necessary drive. He was more important to me then on those cold, dismal days of late fall and early winter than he ever had been for he was my sole companion, regardless of age. And, I had time for no one else.

XXIII

That winter was particularily cold, which made my travels to school nearly unbearable. Still, no matter how sharply the wicked winds cut through me, I walked to school every day. On the days that it snowed I would stop off at Melvin Howard's house to help him shovel his driveway and to share a cup of hot chocolate with him before heading home to shovel my own driveway.

It was during this icy, wintery time that the new neighbors moved in next door to us. The giant Mayflower truck pulled up early on a Saturday morning over my Christmas vacation. Aside from owning what seemed like an awful lot of furniture, this new family had three children: two boys and a girl. The girl was a few years older than me, but from my window, I could tell that the one boy was possibly my age. He was short and frail with longish hair that seemed to hang in his eyes. He looked quiet and intelligent. Up till this point, I had been the only kid on the street in secondary school.

The new neighbors spent the whole day moving in. The moving truck never seemed to empty, and I wondered if my family were to move would we own that much. But, I didn't spend much time considering this because my family had lived in the same house for better than sixteen years. My father's job was stable with no possibility of being transferred so moving to a new neighborhoood in a new town would not happen.

I found out at lunch that day that my father had gone next door to introduce himself to the new neighbors and to offer his help if they needed it.

"The new folks next door seem like interesting people," said my father in a tone of voice that to me seemed to indicate an air of relief. He hung his jacket in the hall closet, rubbed his hands together to shed the chill that had turned them pink, and joined my mother and I at the table for our lunch of grilled cheese and tomato soup.

"He's a professor at Bowling Green. Physics, I think, is what he said," continued my father with his 'state of the new neighbors report.' "I believe he said that his wife is an accountant, but she is looking for a job right now

112

because of the move."

"What are their names?" asked my mother.

"Ah," paused my father, "Forester. That's it. I was thinking Foster at first, but their last name is Forester."

"Well, I can't just call them both Forester, can I?" asked my mother scolding and shaking her head.

"No. His name is Brad and his wife's name is Cheryl; however, I did not meet her."

My father stopped and spooned into his soup and then reached for the package of soda crackers. He never ate soup without crushing crackers over the top. I ate mine plain, but for now, I wasn't really eating because I was interested in hearing my father say more about our new neighbors. Unfortunately, I would have waited for a long time if it weren't for my mother's prompting questions; which meant that my father really did not know much else.

"Did they say where they came from originally?"

"Oh yes," he started again, speaking around a bite of grilled cheese sandwich. (Parents could always talk with food in their mouths. Somehow that behavior was only offensive for children.) "They have been several places before here. Originally, Brad and Cheryl came from the Pittsburgh area. But, before here they were living just outside of Little Rock, Arkansas. Brad was a professor at a small branch campus there."

My father knew more on the matter than I had figured. Our conversation then dipped into a long silence with the only sounds being the crunch of the sandwiches and the clink of spoons against soup bowls. My mother eventually broke the silence as she drained her own soup bowl and rose up from the table to carry her dishes over to the sink to rinse them off.

"Well, that's good that they are nice," she raised her voice over the running water. "I was worried about that." She probably was worried about this too.

"Yeah, he seemed all right," said my father reassuring her.

Still, I waited for my father to say more. He, however, did not. I wanted to say something about the Forester children, namely the boy who I felt was my age. It was an odd interest for me actually because generally I wasn't anxious to find friends. This was rather obvious though since I had no friends except for Melvin Howard. But, I also knew that I wanted friends. After all, it wasn't me that had chosen my social situation. Instead it had been decided for me by peers that really did not want to understand me. And, maybe the boy next door was my chance for a new start.

"I noticed that the Foresters have children too," said my mother. She seemed to always come through whenever I needed her. Maybe she was telepathic and knew what I was thinking.

"Yes, Mr. Forester said that he has four children. One goes to college at Georgetown on scholarship." Then my father smiled directly at me and said, "That is a great school, Martin. Hard to get into."

I just nodded acknowledging him and smiling to indicate that he certainly was right about this. By agreeing I was successful in dodging another conversation about how to motivate me to do better in school.

"I only saw three children, dear, and none of them looked old enough for college," stated my mother further encouraging my father to speak. I merely nodded. I felt like I was doing a lot of nodding which made me feel peculiar.

"Their daughter is in high school and they have two boys. The oldest is your age, Martin."

"Really?" I asked conversationally.

The question was directed at my father, yet it was my mother who chimed in. "Isn't that wonderful?" she said.

I had to respond. Indeed the coincidence was good, but "wonderful"? That was far too hard to be sure of. I did answer though, and I answered positively. I nodded my head "yes", feeling peculiar again. Only this time the peculiar feeling that came over me was not because of my idiotic nodding but because I could already predict the events soon to follow: My mother would press the issue to get me to become friends with this neighbor boy. Mothers can be like that. Not only do they notice everything like the fact that I had really no friends, but she could be almost at times too forceful in trying to help discover what was best for me.

Then, warning or not, the questioning demand came from her. "Martin, perhaps you could walk to school with this new boy?"

She was right. I could, but she failed to ask if I really wanted to try being friends. Of course, I wanted to, but I just thought that she could have considered my interests. I knew she meant nothing by this, yet it still bothered me a little.

"Well, Martin, you could go over there and meet him," said my mother as if everything were all settled. She didn't understand at all. I wanted to make friends, but I wanted to make them in my own way at my own pace. I was never very good at just saying "hello" to a stranger. With this in mind, I decided to wait until I met this new boy by chance.

That afternoon I had to take the garbage out, and an opportunity for me to meet my new neighbors on my own presented itself. The boy who was my age was reluctantly helping his father carry some awkwardly shaped boxes into their garage. All I would have had to do was go over to their house and say "hi" and welcome them to the area; however, I didn't budge. In fact, I could hardly look over at them for fear that he might say something to me first, indicating that this newcomer was far more out-going than I might ever hope to be. Instead, I finished my task of emptying the garbage and dashed back into the house feeling pathetic, stupid, and even lonely.

I stood inside the doorway safe from any contact with my new neighbors, but I hated myself for behaving the way I had. I loathed my social awkwardness, and I wished terrible things upon myself all in an instant. I wanted to be a different person, I wanted to start life over, I wanted to be dead.

There is no one more critical of his own behavior than an adolescent. Being an adolescent, I did not hold back at all in my judgment of myself. The internal wounds that I inflicted upon myself over this were far too deep to be ignored and far too convincing. I had to change. Adults were usually outgoing, so I knew I had to start taking the necessary steps in this direction. But, adolescents are not yet adults, so instead, I summoned up the child in me. I cried.

The next day I went to Melvin Howard's to shovel his driveway because snow had fallen again overnight. For some reason I was so ashamed with myself that I didn't even want to tell Melvin Howard about it. I especially did not want to tell him about how I had pitied myself to the point of tears because I was additionally ashamed now of crying over my shyness. I already felt miserable enough; yet I managed to paint an even worse picture by attaching "silliness" to the already long list of criticisms that I had managed to whip myself with. As I scooped up snow from Melvin Howard's driveway I puzzled over my situation. I had to find an answer to my difficulty with shyness. It was easy to think while I worked because the snow that had fallen was light and powdery and not very hard to clear. This cleared the way for me to think, an activity that did sometimes cause me great strain.

I cleared the driveway very quickly because my mind was distracted from the work just enough to keep me from feeling overburdened. But, it was as I scraped away the last shoveful of snow that my thoughts had culminated enough to give me an answer that was fitting. The idea I came to was not, however, solely my own; but instead, Melvin Howard had helped me out with it two months ago when I confided in him about my crush on Andria. Melvin Howard had been right before. I could say "hello" again. It was, after all, a harmless word that some people even risked using several times daily. I had to teach myself to be stronger. Besides, saying "anything" to Andria was different. I believed her to be my emotional rescue. This neighbor boy was not someone I was trying to fall in love with. No, he was just another boy; maybe even just like me: awkward yet imaginative, a baseball fan who could not really play the sport very well, and even an admirer of pretty, young girls that he was also too afraid to talk to.

I finished the driveway and went inside to have my traditional cup of hot chocolate with Melvin Howard. He always rewarded me with hot chocolate, five dollars, and usually a story for a job well done. It seemed to be a fair trade because the work, even though it was work, was really never very difficult. Melvin Howard, himself, never helped me with the shoveling because he said that when he was in the army he had thrown his back out falling into a fox hole. He said that the cold weather sometimes made his back ache again. 'Besides,' he once said, 'the doctor says that working in cold weather could be bad for my ticker.' He was probably right since he was actually an "old man" despite the fact that I did not really think of him as being very old since we had become friends. Plus, the idea of Melvin Howard even having to see a doctor for any reason just did not seem right, so I gladly shoveled the drive and did not concern myself with Melvin Howard's "ticker."

On my way home from Melvin Howard's, my thoughts returned to saying "hello" to the new neighbor boy. My shyness urged me to devise a few plans, all of which were completely ridiculous. I quickly discarded all of my plans then; except the one that while it did not seem to be the easiest one for me to carry out was actually the most logical. I could just go over to his house and knock on the door and introduce myself to him.

I got home and stepped inside the door when as luck would have it my mother called out from some other room in the house: "Is that you, Martin?" I always wanted to laugh every time she asked me that question when she was home alone. I certainly was an overly shy teenager, but quietly I hoped that I was not as naive as my own mother. Her question also made me want to respond wickedly: "No, ma'am, I'm a psychopathic maniac, and you're my next victim!"

"Martin?" I had pondered too long, and she was growing impatient with the fact that there was another presence in the house with her that failed to have the decency to identify itself properly.

"Hi Mom," I yelled back to her.

"Oh, good," she said emerging from the laundry room or some other place that needed cleaning or organizing in the basement. "You scared me."

"Sorry."

"Now that you're home, could you go out to shovel our driveway, dear?"

My boots were already off but that did not make a difference. I sat back down and tugged my boots back on. My feet suddenly felt very cold.

"Thanks. I told your father that you would. He called."

For some reason, I felt then that I had just won a bet for her that she had had with Dad. The whole idea of my parents holding wagers over whether or not I did my house chores made me chuckle a little. My mother noticed.

"What's so funny, Martin?" She wasn't scolding me. She was curious and little did she know. Besides, she would think I was being silly again. My sense of humor was something that my mother rarely understood.

"Something Melvin Howard told me today," I lied.

"Well, you'll have to tell me the whole story at lunch when you finish up with the driveway. And, Martin?"

"Yes, Mom?" I looked up at her for her last piece of motherly advice before she turned me out into the harsh, cold world of winter and the responsibility of shoveling the drive.

"Really, I wish you wouldn't be so disrespectful." Now, she was scolding. She thought that it was wrong that I never referred to Melvin Howard as "Mr. Howard" any more.

"I'm sorry, Mom, but he doesn't want me to call him 'Mr. Howard'." Now, I told the truth. Melvin Howard always felt that much of the world hid behind titles and the respect that they demanded from others. This, he felt, was why the world could be so confusing and impersonal. 'There are a lot of Mr. Howards in the world, but I want to be myself,' Melvin Howard would say. "It doesn't matter, dear. He's just being nice," returned my mother. "You give him the respect he deserves. After all, he is your boss."

And she thought I was silly at times. Melvin Howard did not seem like a boss. He was my friend. A boss was like Mr. Slate on "The Flintstones'; selfish, intolerant, and never appreciative of his workers. Melvin Howard was none of those things. Furthermore, if Melvin Howard were anything at all, he was a giver, and I felt even that sometimes he gave too much to me because I wasn't that efficient as a worker and usually he helped me with some of the chores. But, the most work I ever did was listen to him which was never difficult.

It was at that moment that it first occurred to me. Melvin Howard needed my friendship as much as I needed his. That's what my chief purpose for him was. This idea that somebody needed me for a friend got my blood flowing again. My confidence was definitely building. Somebody else needed me for a friend, and it could happen again. Having my boots on again and feeling suddenly much warmer, I waved 'good-bye' to my mother and stomped outside into the snow to take on my own driveway. Next door, another boy, bundled up in winter clothing like me, reluctantly pushed a shovel up and down his own driveway. My chance had come and this time would be different because like my mother, my shyness had stayed indoors.

Not wanting to appear too obvious, or too desperate, I grabbed my shovel that was propped against the side of the porch where I had left it two days before. Then, like a true veteran of "driveway shoveling" I positioned the shovel blade toward the light coating of snow and quickly scraped away a small, thin path. I worked a second or so more when I realized that my new neighbor had stopped shoveling. He was not finished yet, but he was resting. Dad said that they had lived in Arkansas right before they moved. Maybe Arkansas did not get enough snow because this boy seemed exhausted, and the driveway had hardly been touched. Perhaps he was working under the coercion of a strict mother as I usually thought I was. There was something else that I noticed, however, as I easily scraped away another miniature path in my own driveway. He had noticed me. He was watching me and kept on doing so until he realized that I had seen him looking over. He then wiped his nose with a mitten, heaved out a frosty breath, and went back to work.

Now, however, I stopped. I was sweating even though the temperature was well below freezing. But, I wasn't really sweating because of nerves like I had originally imagined. Instead, I was sweating out of disbelief because I was actually taking initiative. As near as I could recall, this was something I had never really done before. But, there I was with my snow shovel gripped tightly in one hand and my feet clambering over a small, crunchy snow drift that divided our two yards. Before I knew what had really happened, I was standing with both boots firmly planted in the snow of my new neighbor's driveway. What I did next must have really shocked me because ironically

I have come to consider it to be one of the biggest turning points in my whole life. I extended my right gloved hand and said the first risky word, "Hello."

XXIV

My new neighbor's name was Jason. Jason Forester. He seemed very nice, yet he was soft-spoken and allowed me to do nearly all the talking and the questioning. He, luckily for me, was kind enough to answer and to cater to my unrehearsed and not anticipated small talk. My father was right though. Jason would be in my grade. Through my own research, I had found out that he would be registering for classes right after Christmas break had ended. In addition to his going to school, I also found out that my previous observation was correct. He was not very familiar with shoveling snow.

"Well, haven't you seen snow?" I asked.

"Oh sure, I've seen it enough," returned Jason, who spoke with no Southern accent like I had already prepared myself to hear. "We just never lived anywhere where I had to shovel it before."

"Right now, it seems like that's all I ever do—shovel snow!" I said emphatically as I plunged my shovel into the small drift.

"It snows that much here?" He was surprised.

"Sometimes."

At any rate, we were conversing. That small conversation that started with the discussion of weather conditions served as the first dialogue between Jason Forester and me, and it also served as the stepping stone to what would eventually lead to a close friendship. That first day, until my mother called me in for lunch, with Jason was great even though all we did was combine our forces to clear both driveways. Our conversation never seemed to be very important while we worked, but I was sure at that moment that we were compatible as people. For like me, Jason seemed to be shy. With his family moving so often over the last several years, Jason had had no real chances to make close friends. (This was somewhat of an odd thought for me since I had lived in the same house for all my life and I had not established any close friendships either.) He wore glasses that were stainless steel wire frames, not like my own black frames. His glasses made him appear well-

119

educated, or perhaps, intellectual. Mine, I felt, made me just feel awkward; yet if this were really true, Jason Forester never let on. He also seemed interested in what I was saying even if my conversation was just superficial small talk. For once, I had met one of my peers who seemed to react to me normally, as a person, and not as a potential billboard for a "Kick me" sign.

The rest of Christmas break Jason and I spent a considerable amount of time together. We played games like Risk and Monopoly, watched TV, and I showed him around the neighborhood. The greatest thing about my growing friendship with Jason Forester was that even though I had taken the initiative to talk to him first it did not stay that way. This relationship was not one-sided, for Jason called on me as equally as I called on him. Suddenly, it seemed my spare time was completely taken up. Jason and I were spending so much time together that for a time I honestly had forgotten what I used to do with all of my free time.

Of course, each of us had introduced the other to his respective parents. I liked Jason's parents. They always asked me questions about myself which I was always able to answer. Never before had so many people really seemed to take interest in me as a person, someone worthy of conversation, feeling, and information. This new attention did wonders for my self-esteem. But, this attention toward me didn't stop at the Forester household. It also extended itself to my own home. My parents liked Jason and felt that somehow he might be a good influence on me. In fact, my mother always asked about what Jason and I were up to. My father asked too, especially at the dinner table, where before the conversation was usually about his work day. Also, I had more stock with my own family because I was the link between our house and the Forester house. It was through me that Jason and his whole family first came to dinner at our house. Happily for me, the Foresters and my parents got along quite well. My life was improved with each day Jason Forester and I spent together. Suddenly, I, Martin Hovrick, was somebody. I was important elsewhere besides my own home. For the first time, I was really sure of this. Now, I knew why friendships were so important. Friendship lent purpose to what would normally have been a drab Christmas break. Friendship gave me finally a reason to want to go to school. I felt like I had worth, and that anyone who looked upon me now without realizing this too would surely be blind or just plain ignorant. Instinctively, I had discovered another concept about friendship, and that is that it should be shared. Not only should it be shared equally between the two friends, but it should be expanded to involve other friends. So, I knew it was time before Jason and I began the new year and a new school semester together as friends to introduce him to my other eternal friend, Melvin Howard.

XXV

Melvin Howard came to the door carrying a glass of grapefruit juice, and he saluted me with it upon recognizing me.

"Hello, Martin. How are you?"

"Fine sir."

"Well, come in," Melvin Howard encouraged. I could tell Melvin Howard's attention was now diverted to Jason who had been standing shyly behind me.

"Who's this you have with you, Martin?" asked Melvin Howard once the three of us had stepped into the house.

"Melvin Howard, this Jason Forester. He's my new neighbor," I said proudly.

Melvin Howard extended his hand to my new friend and said, "Welcome Jason. It's good to meet you."

"Thank you Mr. Howard," replied Jason.

"Martin has said a lot about you." I wasn't sure if this were really accurate, yet it probably was since I had spent considerable time preparing Jason for this visit. I wanted the two of them to like each other as much as I liked the two of them.

"All right," said Melvin Howard. "Let's go on into the family room and have a seat. How about a cup of hot chocolate?"

"Sure," I replied.

Melvin Howard turned into the kitchen to prepare the hot chocolate while I showed Jason into the family room, the scene which had been the scene of many of my conversations with Melvin Howard, including my first meeting with him.

In the family room there was a big, warm fire blazing and crackling in the fireplace just like the one that had been burning the day I had first talked to Melvin Howard. Now, here I was introducing Jason to Melvin Howard under the same circumstances. Jason and I both sat on the soft, fluffy couch that slumped against one wall. Melvin Howard would undoubtedly come back to sit in his Lazy-Boy recliner like he always did. Jason's eyes wandered around the cluttered but comfortable room, and I could not help but wonder if his eyes saw the same things that I saw. Eventually I noticed that Jason's eyes had fixed upon the gigantic marlin mounted over the fireplace.

He nudged me. "That's a big fish."

"Yeah," I said. "Melvin Howard caught it in the Caribbean."

"Really?" Jason seemed surprised that anyone would be able to catch a fish that big.

"Really," I returned not surprised by the size of the fish any longer, for I had come to know the creature's captor, Melvin Howard, whom I believed could make nearly anything possible.

Melvin Howard came back into the living room carrying a tray of three steaming mugs. Melvin Howard always made his own hot chocolate rather than the instant kind. He always felt that instant anything was just another way for society to cut corners. In so doing, he felt this practice could only eventually lead to sacrificed quality. This attitude of Melvin Howard's seemed somewhat old-fashioned, but I never disagreed. Plus, I was never any less appreciative for the hot chocolate.

Once all three of us had taken a mug, Melvin Howard settled back into his recliner, blew some of the steam off his hot chocolate, and took a sip, slurping a bit as he did.

"So, Jason, where are you from originally?" Melvin Howard quizzed, his crystal blue eyes focusing on Jason.

"Well, we've moved a lot of times, but I was born in Philadelphia."

Melvin Howard nodded and smiled. "Is that where you just moved from?"

"No," replied Jason shaking his head and trying to swallow some hot chocolate all in the same motion. "We just moved here from Little Rock," Jason said.

"Arkansas?" This time Melvin Howard's eyes locked on me. "You ever been to Arkansas, Martin?"

"No, sir," I smiled back. I was anticipating what would probably be the inevitable—a Melvin Howard story.

"It's a beautiful state. Not a lot of people really, but it's beautiful."

"Really?" I asked.

"Yes, did Jason tell you that Arkansas is called the Diamond State?"

"No."

"It is?" asked Jason. "I didn't know that." This made Melvin Howard chuckle a little.

"Well, supposedly it's the only state in the union where diamonds can actually be mined, however, I don't think finding them is real common." Melvin Howard stopped and sipped his hot chocolate. I copied him.

"How do you like it here in beautiful Ohio so far, Jason?"

"So far I guess it isn't that bad," shrugged Jason. "I really only know Martin so far, and he seems really nice. We've been having fun together."

I blushed at Jason's awkward compliment and tried to hide behind my hot chocolate cup. Compliments, while they are nice, sometimes made me more uncomfortable than when someone criticized me.

"Well, that's good," said Melvin Howard happily. "Martin needs to meet some decent friends and you two should get along fine. " Melvin Howard nodded at me to which I acknowledged with a sheepish smile, still trying to ward off the slight embarrassment caused by Jason's compliments.

"Yes, coming to a new place can be easier by making friends right away." Jason and I looked at each other over our mugs. We had become friends, and I knew that Jason was as glad about our friendship as I was. And now, the friendship between Jason and I had the blessing of my greatest friend, Melvin Howard. I was not really sure as to why I felt it was so important that Melvin Howard approve of my friendship with Jason, for I was still learning so much about what friendships really were. Perhaps I respected his judgment and was really still a little under-confident about my own, or maybe I wanted the chance to share something of my life and own initiative with Melvin Howard. But, also, I couldn't help but wonder what affect my friendship with Jason would have on my friendship with Melvin Howard. I knew that while I did not want to forget about either one of them, I also knew that sharing them could prove to be difficult where my feelings were concerned. Instead of dwelling on the subject, I sipped my now-cooling hot chocolate and again focused in on the conversation of the moment. I could not help but notice that Jason was again staring, amazed at the marlin. This time Melvin Howard noticed as well.

"He's a big fella, isn't he?"

"Huh?" asked Jason. Quite honestly, Melvin Howard's sudden question startled me too for I was also staring at the marlin. I had actually come to take the big fish for granted.

"He fought like hell too," said Melvin Howard cockily and shaking his head at the memory. I remembered the story he had told me one rainy afternoon about catching the marlin. It had been a good story.

"It was in the early 1950's, and my wife and I had gone with another couple to the Caribbean, The Bahamas actually for vacation. . . .'

XXVI

In the early dawn Melvin Howard rose hurriedly and splashed his face with water from a bedside basin to revive him from a restless sleep. He slept the kind of sleep Columbus might have slept the night before he set sail for the Americas. Today Melvin Howard was in search of adventure. Spontaneously he and his close friend, co-worker, and now traveling companion decided yesterday to take a stab at deep sea fishing when they saw one of the charter boats return from one such trip. In the haul, Melvin saw plenty of grouper, a dolfin, and a giant hammerhead shark.

Melvin Howard's friend Al Stanley, a lanky man with a casual Ohio accent whistled when he saw the crew unload the hammerhead. Growing up with smallmouth bass and channel cats, the two men stood in marked amazement at the size of the fish.

"Damn," was all Al could manage and he whistled through his teeth again.

In the next instant, the two men were at dockside inquiring about the next charter. Money did not seem to matter even though Melvin knew that this expedition would be expensive. Neither of the men had even checked it with their respective wives before reserving a spot on the next charter to deep sea adventure. Permission did not seem to be needed thought Melvin for he knew his wife would understand. She usually did. She was probably a saint in reality. Al's wife, on the other hand, was more particular about the spontaneity with which Al went about planning his excursions of male bonding.

Still, Al lived for Al, and Al lived for the moment. Inspired by the excitement of possibly hooking a shark or maybe a marlin, the two jubilantly signed up and then explained their plans to their wives. Al had to warm his wife up to the idea while Melvin was able to come right out with it. Eventually, the ladies agreed that being away from their husbands might be adventurous in its own right because they could go into Nassau to shop in all of the curio stores without feeling rushed.

After kissing his sleeping wife gently, Melvin and Al met in the hotel lobby before walking the short distance down to the dock to meet the charter boat.

"Howdy Mel. You ready to go get 'em?" Al beamed from ear to ear.

"You bet!" Melvin was eager too.

"Let's get some coffee first."

The two men walked into the cafe and ordered. Melvin ordered his coffee black while Al asked for some sugar for his. As he put it: "Hot as hell and sweet as an angel." Al was blunt and uncultured, but Melvin found him entertaining. Al's customers at the insurance agency back home saw Al's bluntness as honesty and his being uncultured as being a "down home boy".

The two men sipped their coffee hurriedly, trying not to inflict third degree burns upon their tongues. Both of them talked excitedly about the upcoming day's events. They hoped out loud about making "the big catch" that might not only give them bragging rights back home but possibly even launch them into some local record books here in the Bahamas. Both men easily visualized a snapshot in their heads of themselves, smiling next to a gigantic shark or some other monstrous creature from the deep. They were like two children sharing stories of anticipated Christmas gifts.

Slurping the last of his coffee, Al stood up and clapped Melvin on the back.

"You ready, Mel? Time to saddle up."

"I'm right behind you," announced Melvin also swigging down his last gulp.

When Melvin and Al stepped out to meet the day, the sun was just starting to break through the early morning haze that snugly covered the islands overnight. Clutching their gear that mainly consisted of suntan lotion, mosquito repellent, and a couple changes of clothes, the two men strode toward the docks like warriors to battle. Ahead of them was the charter boat. It was nothing pretty to look at but for its purposes it didn't have to be. The two men barely noticed the boat's appearance save for the fact that it was definitely the boat that would take them far out to sea, a place from which they would not return until approximately nightfall.

Once they stepped onto the boat, Melvin and Al were greeted by the first mate of the charter, Hank Green. Hank looked like a typical seaman. He wore a dingy white sailor's skull cap pulled down tight over greasy, unkempt hair. The dark stubble on his chin was just as greasy looking as his hair and gave him the appearance of a criminal. On one burly bicep Hank had a tattoo of a rose and on the forearm of the opposite arm he brandished a tattoo of a black panther. There was no way to tell the age of this seafarer by appearance alone because his face was so torn with scars and was so weather-beaten that he was hopefully much younger than he looked. With such a surly look about him, Melvin thought it was odd that it was Hank who was checking off the names and passing out the affidavits for the oncoming passengers.

"Fill this form out after you read it," grunted Hank gritting his teeth against a toothpick. Melvin took the form and quickly skimmed the fine print of the affidavit and signed it with the pen that Hank had also provided for him. Al then did the same; thus, relieving the charter of all liability just in case anything should go wrong while at sea.

The boat had benches for possibly fifteen to twenty men to fish at once. The charter company provided a lunch, bait, line, and most importantly the large, heavy poles used in deep sea fishing. These poles made the cane pole that Melvin grew up using to catch bullhead in the Blanchard River look like nothing more than a stick. The technology and the innovation that had obviously gone into the development of such a pole did not seem to give the fish any chance at all. From first glance, these special deep sea rods looked as if they could do nearly everything for the fisherman except put the fish on the hook. But, once a fish did bite one of the fist-sized hooks there was little chance for escape thought Melvin. The poles had so much play in them that even the toughest fighter would have a rough time getting free again. The toughness of these deep sea creatures, however, was not something that Melvin could accurately estimate. Being new to deep sea fishing, he was naive to the strength these gigantic fish actually possessed and that the real reason for such a heavy duty pole was to just make catching one of the giants possible.

Once all of the passengers reserved for the expedition were on board, the boat motored its way out of the harbor and into the open water. The journey to the designated fishing spot would take a little over an hour, so Melvin and Al just sat back to enjoy the ride. The waves were slight and the ride was smooth. It would be a beautiful day to be on the ocean, according to the captain. Melvin was so anxious to get started with the actual fishing that he wanted to drop anchor right away and cast off; however, just like fishing along the Blanchard, Melvin assumed that some spots were better than others. The captain, a clone of Hank Green, had assured the passengers aboard that the spot they were heading for would prove to be "good fishing".

It did not take long for the boat to be completely away from land, and Melvin felt very alone and at peace—almost too much at peace. The feeling gave him an interesting picture that allowed him to imagine himself in his own after life, completely shut off from the world as he knew it, coasting or drifting through what resembled eternity, searching for a point somewhere in this empty tranquility. The image of the after life bothered him and he quickly discontinued his train of thought. All he really needed to concentrate on was the task at hand. The sport of fishing gripped him and he suddenly wondered what he would do if he caught anything. Would he eat the fish or would he mount it? Mounting could be interesting, and Melvin could easily picture the figure of a giant blue marlin mounted over his mantle. This image helped cast a satisfied and determined smile across Melvin's face. Even though he would be taking this beautiful trophy from Nature, he decided that he liked this latter image better than his prior one about the after life. After all, Melvin felt that it would be better to take a little from Nature than to succumb to Nature.

"We sure are a long way out." Al's voice startled Melvin from his dream state.

"Yeah," began Melvin slowly. "The captain said that it might take at least an hour to get out far enough."

"Right. I wonder how far that is in miles," Al rolled his eyes trying to logically think up a solution to his own question.

"I'm not sure," Melvin surrendered.

"Me neither." Al quit too. It was definitely not a day for thought. After all, so much of sport was purely reaction, and for now, Melvin stared out at the horizon merely reacting. Everything in sight was blue and bright, and that everlasting image of eternity slowly crept back before Melvin. They were a long way out, and he felt uncomfortably relaxed.

Finally the motor of the boat sputtered and ceased. The boat continued to float gently in the current that had lightly played with the hull of the fishing boat throughout the trip. All around Melvin and Al men started moving about, talking excitedly, and stretching after the hour-long journey. The spot at which the boat had arrived was situated neatly between nowhere and nothing. Everywhere around them was the vivid blue that had accompanied them throughout the trip; but nevertheless, they had finally arrived. In this vast blue playground stretching from one horizon to the next, Melvin and Al would attempt to meet adventure and what they hoped would not elude them—the prized trophy fishes that both men hoped these waters would yield.

The sweat popped out on Melvin's forehead and ran down over his nose where a droplet hung until he could wipe it away with his shirt sleeve. Melvin leaned back, sighed, and relaxed the grip he had on the fishing pole. The sun was hot, and Melvin could feel the sunburn just starting on his face. It had been two hours since he and Al had first cast off and so far neither of them had caught anything.

Melvin looked over at Al. He had his Ohio State baseball cap pulled down low over his eyes, and for a moment, Melvin actually thought that Al might be asleep. Yet, as Melvin thought this, Al also sighed and turned to his friend. "Damn it! That sun is really hot."

"You even had a nibble yet?" asked Melvin.

"Hell no," swore Al. He was getting impatient. "Now, I know why I like fishing for bass. You don't have to wait forever to get a bite."

Normally, patience is a virtue, especially in the fisherman's case, however, this never held true for Al. Al was perhaps impatient by nature for he was that way at work as well. Often times, he was a pushy salesman who would not take no for an answer. Melvin, on the other hand, at work wasn't as concerned with just making the sale. Instead, he was also concerned with his customer's satisfaction. He went into insurance because he thought that he could help others who were going through unfortunate times or were trying to avoid such times. Either way, Melvin's success in the business had come from patience and understanding. Melvin always thought that since insurance played such an important role in most people's lives it was better to have them satisfied completely rather than forced into making a hasty decision.

As a fisherman, Melvin never minded the waiting because he enjoyed fishing in order to relax. There were not many smallmouth bass in Melvin's favorite childhood fishing spot but there was relaxation. Going to the pond was always a chance for Melvin to go some place else for a short time. Actually catching fish seemed secondary to unwinding.

Melvin and Al were different in many of their methods, but regardless, they were friends and always supported the other one's style of doing business or appreciating life.

"Hey, Melvin! Mel!" shouted Al standing up excitedly from his chair.

Melvin snapped out of his moment of self-analysis to see Al fighting with his fishing pole that was jerking and snapping like a whip. Al pulled back his shoulders and the rod bent considerably. The hook had definitely attached itself to something, and whatever it was did not want to be caught.

"Give him some more line," coached Melvin. Melvin's own adrenaline was pumping through his body. The creature on the other end of Al's line was fixing to be a fighter.

Al gave the fish more line to run with and as soon as the fish had begun to swim further out to sea at what seemed like amazing speed Al fought to turn it back toward the boat.

"Come on Al!" encouraged Melvin. "You've got him. Don't let up."

The fish on Al's hook was very strong and definitely was not a smallmouth bass. Again, Al lurched his shoulders backward to tug the deep sea monster in while the fish reciprocated by trying to head back out to sea. Man vs Nature, one of the all-time classic confrontations. Melvin reeled his own line in while trying to coach Al to victory, for Al now seemed to be involved in the toughest tug-o-war match of his life.

"Al, sit down." Melvin buckled Al into his seat to help provide him with more leverage. Once seated, Al could rely more on his arm strength since he could maintain better balance. Again, Al let the line out, toying with the fish. The line again started to dart out to sea, but Al expertly and quickly brought the line back in. Hopefully this practice might eventually tire the fish out.

Several other men had now put down their poles too and came over to help Al hold onto the pole. He definitely had a big one hooked for the pole was bending into a near perfect arc. Melvin grabbed the pole with Al to steady it and to add to the advantage of more leverage.

"You just concentrate on reeling him in Al," shouted Melvin out of excitement. Al's only acknowledgement was grabbing the reel. Together the two men fought against the fighter at the other end of the hook, and together they made progress until suddenly the vivid blue sea turned frothy in one spot about forty yards out and erupted, spouting up a giant white splash followed by the leaping, long, slender, silvery body of a writhing fish.

"Cuda," said one of the other men grimly.

Al let the barracuda have more line, and the sinister fish leaped high into the air again, at which time Melvin yanked back firmly on the rod. This fish was not going to get away.

"Keep with it, Al," pushed Melvin. Al whinced and reeled the fish a little further in. Barracudas, however, can fight like the very Devil himself as the captain had mentioned at the start of the trip, and these waters were loaded with them. But, for now, only one barracuda mattered, and Al was looking tired. Together, he and Melvin pulled back on the rod forcing the fish in closer. The strain on the tip of the rod was remarkable, and Melvin thought that it would surely break. Al's forearms tightened as he managed to again drag the "cuda" closer to which the fish responded by bursting from the water again. It was a strenuous battle; however, the fish now did not seem to be leaping as high. He would tire soon perhaps.

"That's it Al! He's getting tired. You've got him," Melvin said lurching backward simultancously with Al. Al's cap had long since slid from his head. The sweat covered both men, stinging their eyes to temporary blindness; yet they did not need eyes to battle this fish. They could feel he was still there in every muscle fiber, pulling against them. This type of fishing was definitely a sport, and Melvin knew that Al had to be getting tired for Melvin himself from just steadying the rod and coaching Al even felt the burden of the struggle. Their pain and effort would not go without reward. The barracuda leaped again, but this time his leap was feeble. He was assuredly wearing down. Al was going to catch a barracuda and Melvin was glad.

XXVII

Well over an hour had passed since Al had finally landed the barracuda. Melvin decided that never before had he seen such an evil-looking creature. There was only one purpose for barracudas, according to the captain, and that was to attack anything. The fish is exceptionally aggressive and judging from the many razor sharp teeth that stood out from its ugly, protruding lower jaw, Melvin could fully understand what the captain meant. This particular barracuda was about five feet long and weighed close to eighty pounds. Al had decided to mount the fish. Melvin could see the beautiful trophy hanging in Al's den at home. Melvin could also visualize Al admiring it for long moments each day, longing to tell the story of its capture over and over.

Melvin then decided to cast out again since the boat had quieted after the excitement of Al's catch. Al had not yet returned to his seat for he had gone below deck for a beer. The "cuda" had worn him out. Actually, Melvin felt tired too, but he still had enough energy to try for a trophy fish of his own.

The line floated through the air and dropped into the water about fifty yards out. The sun was still high in the sky and scorching. Unlike Al, Melvin was not wearing a hat, a practice he had never gotten used to. As a boy, Melvin seldom wore even a baseball cap. Now, however, he was wishing that he had worn something, for the sun beating on the top of his head was starting to make his scalp itch and perspire uncomfortably.

Still, Melvin settled in for the anxious waiting that would accompany this cast. For the first time as a fisherman, Melvin felt impatient and the feeling irritated him a little. Fishing was one of the only sports that depended heavily on luck as well as skill. The fisherman could have the best equipment and the bait best-suited for capturing the finest fish, yet unless, one fish took the bait, the fisherman had literally no say in the outcome. Melvin did not allow his thoughts to stray to the horizon at all. Instead, he kept a steady eye on the tip of his rod, waiting for even a hint of a nibble. In the heat, his eyes even played tricks on him as he wanted so badly to see the line tug. The old cliche of the watched pot never boiling came to mind, but Melvin's eyes did not stray from the tip of the rod. He waited, sweating, almost wishing; but the line never jumped.

Another half hour or so had passed, and the sun had now climbed past its noon time summit beginning its descent toward the west. Al had finally returned and clapped Melvin's shoulder, startling him.

"Sorry, Mel. Didn't mean to scare you."

Melvin recovered from the surprise of Al's return and turned, squinting against the sun. "That's all right, Al."

"Hey, thanks a lot for your help with that fish," said Al sincerely. "I couldn't have done it without you."

"Don't worry about it," shrugged Melvin, his eyes returning again to the tip of his rod. Still nothing.

"I think I'll mount that big, ugly fish," said Al kicking back in his chair and closing his eyes to the bright sun.

"What?" Melvin had heard Al's voice, but he really was not paying attention to him.

"Oh," Al paused. "Nothing, just bragging about my fish."

Melvin just laughed at this. Al certainly was the most straightforward guy Melvin had ever met. Al snickered too and took out a toothpick. Al probably did not have anything in his teeth, but he just liked to chew on toothpicks, a habit to which he took like a chainsmoker to cigarettes. Melvin thought Al's toothpick chewing was a silly habit even though it did not really bother him. Melvin just had a difficult time understanding what pleasure exactly Al derived from chewing the toothpicks. The idea of Al being addicted to the taste of wood always struck Melvin as funny.

"Doesn't it figure," said Al rolling his toothpick and then pausing to spit out a piece of the wood. (At least he didn't eat the wood too, thought Melvin.) "of all the fish in the ocean, I catch one of the ugliest ones."

Al was never satisfied, but Melvin laughed any way.

"I don't know," smiled Melvin, one eye watching the rod and one on Al. "I think somehow it's fitting."

Al laughed hard. "You wish, pal."

"Really, you keep chewing those toothpicks your bottom jaw will probably look like that too," teased Melvin.

"Hey! C'mon now...," Al started to defend himself again but stopped in mid-sentence. "Hey! Mel, you got a bite!"

Melvin, startled, tried to re-group. Al was right. The end of the rod had begun to bob just a little. Whatever was at the other end was just nibbling at the bait. For the moment, there was no guarantee that the fish would even bite down on the hook. So, Melvin had to wait impatiently. His adrenaline was pumping, waiting for the right moment to pull back on the rod. Melvin could feel Al standing very close to him now. Al anticipated the same moment that Melvin awaited. First, there would be a big tug on the line and then Melvin would yank the rod back to secure the hook. Second, the fight would begin. After seeing Al's battle with the barracuda, Melvin was more than mentally ready for the struggle. Although he was still physically drained from helping Al land his trophy, Melvin was anxious for the fight to begin.

"Don't lose him, Mel," said Al drawing out his words cautiously. But, Melvin knew it was hard to lose what one does not have.

"I won't," uttered Melvin gritting his teeth firmly. It was not a time for philosophy.

The seconds propelled themselves into minutes that seemed to drag for a millenium, but still, Melvin knew he needed to be patient. If he rushed now the fish nibbling at the bait might never even take it. Then all of Melvin's efforts would be spent for nothing. Timing was everything since mere seconds were the difference between victory and defeat, success and failure.

Then just as subtly as the nibble, the rod began to slowly bow downward. The fish was taking the bait. At first, the pulling was slow and gentle, giving the illusion to Melvin that the fish might not really be that big. However, just when Melvin thought this, his hidden deep sea opponent made its true strength felt.

"Good God!" yelled Al as he too saw the rod bend close to the breaking point. Melvin could not respond. He was settling in for the ensuing battle. The physical fatigue from helping Al had disappeared. Melvin now braced and tightened his arms and planted his feet firmly. Al wasted no time buckling Melvin into his seat in case the ride got wild.

Again, the rod bent decisively. It was time. 'Man vs Nature'. Hemingway's words flashed quickly through Melvin's mind. When he had first read those words they did not matter. But, now here, in the thick of the action, the relationship was simple and it clearly spelled out: powerful struggle.

Melvin quickly and firmly pulled back on the rod. The hook now planted securely in the fish's mouth, Melvin began to play the creature. He let the line out to give the fish room to resist without breaking the line. The fish responded as expected. Almost as soon as the hook found its mark the line seemed to shoot like a launched torpedo toward the open sea.

With Al's help Melvin steadied the rod which shook from the strain. Melvin's previous assumption about the fish not being so large was merely that, an assumption. It soon became obvious that the fish was very strong and probably of exceptional size. If Melvin had not been able to tell this from pulling and struggling, he should have been able to tell from the large throng of men that had suddenly gathered around him.

"That a way, Mel!" cheered Al. "Play him a little more." Melvin accepted Al's coaching and let the line out a bit more. The fish responded by racing further away, straining the line and Melvin's forearms that now seemed just an extension to the rod that his hands gripped in white-knuckled intensity. The competition had only just begun and Melvin's brow already dripped profusely and the fatty part of his hands started to cramp up. Yet, it seemed impossible for him to loosen his grip. The fish retreated again, but Melvin grunted and heaved his shoulders, pulling the fish slightly closer to the boat. The bending rod looked as if it would surely snap before this fish story became a success story. Melvin was one who never enjoyed telling the stories about 'the one that got away.' He did not aim to start telling those types of stories with this fish either.

"C'mon Melvin!"

Melvin was suddenly aware of Al's sweating face right over his shoulder. Al too was intense and to uphold Al's encouragement Melvin braced himself and pulled hard, literally dragging the fish in.

Suddenly then the strain on the line ceased and all was quiet. Melvin knew, however, that the fish had not broken the line because the tip of the rod still bobbed slightly. Perhaps this deep sea monster was surrendering to Melvin Howard and prepared to take its appropriate place alongside the many bullhead and pickerel Melvin had pulled out of the Blanchard as a boy.

But, just as how the quiet of a storm is often followed by the most violent gale, so was this fish's fight. Somehow the fish had gotten its second wind. The second effort surprised Melvin, nearly yanking the pole from his grip. While Melvin anticipated the struggle to continue, he had not been prepared for the fight's quick revival. Fortunately, Al once again helped Melvin get settled. He helped by steadying the rod, which kept it from flying from Melvin's hands and into the ocean.

Melvin's breath burst from behind pursed lips, temporarily alleviating some of the strain that his muscles experienced. Every part of his body seemed to be sweating, and even though he was aware of this, Melvin found the sensation easy to ignore. Instead, he fixed his eyes on the brilliant and sparkling ocean, watching for even a glimpse of the giant that he had hooked. The horizon yielded nothing. The water remained the same rippling plane of blue. And, then the line suddenly took off rapidly nearly unwinding the whole reel. Melvin needed all of his effort, both mental and physical, to regain control of the situation. He had allowed the fish too much room to fight. Now, Melvin would have his work cut out for him for sure. Vaguely, Melvin could hear Al swearing at him for being so careless. To make up for his error in concentration, Melvin began reeling the line back in. Turning the reel was as difficult as trying to turn a stripped screw with a dull Phillip's head, but Melvin fought with the reel. He fought the fish that as of yet he had not seen. He fought with himself inside his own mind. Melvin battled bitterly now with the all too present possibility of failure.

As Melvin continued to arm wrestle with the stubborn reel, Al saw the opportunity and grabbed the rod, allowing Melvin to concentrate solely on reeling. Al would strain against the weight of the fish for awhile until Melvin could even the fight up by lessening the fish's line.

"We got you Mel," shouted Al nearly in Melvin's ear. "Just pull. Pull like hell."

Apparently the extra weight on the rod struck a nerve in Melvin's fish because it was at that moment that the giant blue marlin leapt from the sparkling waves and high into the air. With a huge splash of white, the marlin flopped and crashed back to the sea. Melvin tried not to be too amazed by the size of the fish or by the excitement he felt pulsing through his every pore. Melvin expertly ignored the urge to smile and gloat, trading these sensations for renewed physical strength. With determination, Melvin fought the reel and suddenly seemed to be winning. The line now thrashed from side to side. The marlin raised its head up from the water and seemed to stare Melvin down, but Melvin was sure that he recognized the beginning of surrender in the fish's eyes. Still, Melvin shook it off because it seemed ridiculous to him that a fish could show such expressions. Quickly, Melvin got himself back into the fight .

"Reel Melvin!" Al was still coaching. Al and another man started to heave against the fish as Melvin worked the reel and lifted the rod when he could take a second's break from reeling.

The fish leapt up out of the water once again, and although this jump was considerably more feeble than its previously stunning effort, the marlin was now close enough to shower the boat with the salty spray. The giant was tiring. The fish would soon be conquered, and Al patted Melvin's shoulder, giving Melvin the official victory. For now, all that had to be done was to lift the huge fish from the water which was no easy task due to its immense weight. But, for the time, Melvin allowed his arms to relax. He had gone all fifteen rounds with Nature and he had won. . . .

Melvin Howard's story ended, and the three of us sat long admiring the fish now mounted to the wall above the fireplace. I found it difficult to believe that the fish was really real. Once, according to the story, that fish had jumped from the safety of the sea high into the air. It was hard to imagine except that I then noticed it too. The eyes. The eyes of the marlin were blank and defeated, perhaps, this is what Melvin Howard had imagined upon capturing it. Now, the eyes were permanently fixed with each pupil seemingly waving its own white flag.

As I lost myself in the eyes of the great marlin, I knew the only thing that lived for the moment was the story itself. This thought depressed me a little. This once great creature was shaken down to an arguably unrealistic trophy. Melvin Howard then broke my train of thought and made his point.

"I couldn't have caught that big fella without Al," he said smiling. "Good old Al."

XXVIII

The last half of the school year during eighth grade passed like no other school year before. With Jason around I was a different person. I was more sure of myself and I even spoke to more people. I attributed my social growth at school to the fact that Jason was my close friend. Since Jason was a new student, many students wanted to meet him to find out what he was like. To do this, everyone usually went through me because he seemed to be my friend. Upon meeting Jason, people liked him. My status at school improved immensely, because it was decided that if Jason liked me, I must not be so bad.

Like many other underdogs, I only needed a chance. Once I was given this chance, I made the best of it. I also grew physically. Even though I was still very thin, I had grown a whole four to five inches since the start of school. This unexpected growth spurt had me now up close to five feet eight inches tall and one of the tallest boys in my class, where before I was one of the smallest. Athletically, I was still recognized as having little or no ability, but the other students no longer chose to pick on me. They never picked on Jason either because he was smart and most of the bullies or popular girls needed some help on their homework. Luckily, Jason could provide them with the appropriate help, and it was during these study hall tutor sessions that these other students started to realize my personality as interesting and my imagination as clever.

The surprising thing to me was that since I had become accepted by my peers my grades also improved. I was able to attribute much of this improvement in academics to my friendship with Jason. Jason seemed to enjoy learning and he never seemed satisfied until he could learn more. His example began to rub off on me. We studied together and he quizzed me for tests. My grades mattered to me for the first time in my life. Unlike Jason who realized that performing well in school was directly related to attaining a career later, I found that by getting good grades, I gained respect from Jason. My parents were pretty pleased too. But, I knew that being interested in my grades could assure me of remaining close with Jason.

Plus, Jason was also interested in people and their feelings. It was this characteristic that kept him from being labeled a "book worm". Jason was not exactly popular because he never went out of his way to hang out with the popular kids, however, he initiated conversation with them. He was quiet, yet he was not shy, and he was interested in what others had to say.

Once Jason thanked me for introducing him to some girls during lunch. In reality, the girls had asked to meet Jason. He did not know this. He thought that I had given him an opportunity to make new friends even though I really had very little to do with these opportunities. Still, I let him believe this because feeling responsible for introducing Jason to others made me feel less guilty for receiving all of the good things that he had really done for me.

XXIX

That spring I finally found out what it was like to feel busy. It was as if nobody would let me rest. To me it seemed that my life as a kid was probably over. My parents had me doing yard work at our house nearly every other day in addition to my work at Melvin Howard's house which was gradually became reduced because of my full schedule. Occasionally I still went down the street to mow Mrs. McDaniel's lawn. Despite my outburst that one awful day in her yard, the old lady was just as nagging as ever. I usually passed the time cutting her grass by swearing continuously under my breath. Since swearing was a relatively new, and possibly, risky practice for me, I kept all of these four-letter derogatory comments under my breath and softer than could be detected by Ol' Mrs. McDaniel.

Aside from working outside on the weekends, Jason and I started to spend time at the mall. We never really did anything there, but we were convinced that we were having the greatest time of our young lives. Sometimes we would go see movies together. We could not decide which movie we liked best since there were three that we were fairly partial to: "Star Wars," "Close Encounters," and "Jaws". We were both science fiction fans so the first two were outstanding. But, "Jaws" was an R-rated movie and we sneaked in to see it when the usher was not paying close attention. We had really bought tickets to see Walt Disney's "The Rescuers," and then, we ducked in to see "Jaws". The savage attacks by the giant great white terrified me but because we had gone to so much trouble to see the movie, it will possibly always be one of my favorites. Jason and I both told Melvin Howard about seeing "Jaws" afterward since seeing it reminded us of Melvin Howard's own fishing trip in which he had caught the blue marlin. He commended us on our adventuresome attitudes but also warned us not to make it a practice. Because of Melvin Howard's warning, Jason and I had put off our next R-rated adventure, "Animal House." It was probably for the best though because the only kid that we knew who had actually seen the movie said it was hilarious. However, when he explained one of the memorable scenes to us, I failed to understand the humor. Jason and I were mostly intrigued by the idea that the movie had nudity even if the humor was bound to go over our heads. Nevertheless, we waited, heeding Melvin Howard's warning.

Throughout my young life I was always accustomed to hearing people complain about being busy. I too fell into this practice when it came to doing the yard work dictated by my parents, but the truth was that I really enjoyed having a lot to do. In fact, I could not wait for summer to actually arrive so that I would have even more time to spend. The only sad thing I found about being so busy for myself was that I rarely had enough time to spend with Melvin Howard. This, when I thought of it, was a huge sacrifice for me to make because previously I had placed so much importance on relaxing with him and listening to one of the infinitely interesting stories about his life. Those stories were fewer and farther between now. Usually right after I finished working at Melvin Howard's I rushed home for dinner and then off with Jason. In the past, my mother would not start dinner until I had returned from Melvin Howard's because I never had any other plans. But, my life, however, was decisively and uncontrollably changing. And, as a young teenager, I wanted to please everybody and still please myself, which can often times, be a near impossible task.

What concerned me most was Melvin Howard. I was worried that he would think bad of me for not being able to hear more of his stories. But, even though I could not hear Melvin Howard's stories as often, I still showed up to work at his house religiously. This I never wanted to change. However, one afternoon, a rare afternoon when I did not have to run off immediately, Melvin Howard and I were playing gin rummy because we really did not have much work to do. It was then that I told him how Jason's family had asked me to go with them to the Ohio State Fair.

"Oh, good for you," smiled Melvin Howard over his cards. "You'll love it."

"Oh," was all I could manage.

"You don't seem too thrilled?" asked Melvin Howard.

I shrugged and said, "Well, I can't go."

"Why not?"

This bothered me a little that he was so encouraging because to me the answer was obvious. "Saturdays I come here to help you," I replied quietly.

"Martin?"

"Yes sir."

"Look at me," he said since my eyes were buried deep in my cards. Laying his cards on the table face down, Melvin Howard continued, "You should go. It's really a marvelous time. Marcia and I took the kids several times."

"Well?" I began my eyes questioning, looking for something that might resemble distinct approval while my voice was lax and disinterested.

"Well, I think you should go," demanded Melvin Howard. "Think of it like some sort of vacation. Every employee deserves an occasional vacation." With Melvin Howard's support I was happy. I really did want to go to the fair, and with Melvin Howard's approval, the trip would now be perfect.

We returned to our card game at which Melvin Howard soundly beat me. He usually did since I was just learning gin rummy. When he discarded his last card, Melvin Howard chuckled a little. He always seemed to enjoy winning, and he extended his hand in light of sportsmanship. I took his hand, feeling as if I was somehow thanking him for beating me. We then both sat back and were silent momentarily. I was just going to ask for a rematch when Melvin Howard spoke.

"Martin," he sighed. "Have I ever told you about the time my son, Tom left home for the first time?"

"No sir."

"It was back in 1968, I believe. The Viet Nam War was at full- tilt. . . ."

XXX

The June sun was hot, and Melvin Howard was trying to chase away the heat with an ice cold glass of pink lemonade. He had been doing some menial tasks in the yard; weeding, trimming, and picking up sticks that had fallen from the old maple trees. For now though, Melvin was taking a break. He hated hot, humid days, but the yard work needed to be done. Tom, Melvin's boy, would take time out from his busy schedule to mow the grass later on; so Melvin decided to do some of the touch-up work to make things easier.

Tom recently graduated from high school and like most young men his age was eager to grow up quickly. Seeing the boy now amazed Melvin because he had nearly grown into a full-fledged man from the body of a stocky, bow-legged little kid. Gangling awkwardness had missed Tom and in its place he had developed clean-cut All-American good looks, handsome and strong with a wiry, athletic build. Tom was a letterman as a receiver for the football team and as a miler on the track team. The boy's grades were fair and he was popular, especially with the girls. In fact, Tom Howard never seemed to be without a girlfriend. While Melvin sat thinking of his son, he really only had one criticism: Tom had literally no idea what he was going to do now that he had graduated.

Wiping his brow with his arm, he took one last sip of lemonade and caught one ice cube in his mouth to suck on. Melvin sighed and stood to go back to work when Tom's red Corvair grunted up the driveway. The little sports car sounded more like a power boat than a car, and he often jokingly teased Tom about it. Despite Melvin's ribbing, Tom took great pride in the automobile that he had saved all summer, every summer throughout his teenage life to buy. Melvin had secretly wished that his son would save his money for a college education rather than a car; however, this was not to be. Melvin remembered being inspired by his son's thrifty efforts of saving his earnings from his two jobs just so he could be the first of his immediate friends to buy his own car. Melvin used this inspiration to set his sights on eventually buying a fishing boat which was something that he had always wanted. With his own boat, perch fishing would be much easier. So, Melvin decided to open an additional bank account to which he made small, yet hopeful deposits. That bank account unfortunately had not received any activity for several months, and while Melvin had not lost interest in buying a fishing boat, he had lost interest in dutifully saving for one. So, his "dream ship" had all but capsized even though Melvin would not admit it to himself. In his mind, he was still saving laboriously.

Tom was different. Ever since his childhood, Tom had easily recognized opportunity and then seized it. Tom was gutsy and willing to make sacrifices to make what others might simply call dreams come true. The little red Corvair that Tom proudly cruised the town in was just one example that came to mind. However, Melvin also remembered Tom setting up a Kool-Aid stand in the front yard. At the time, construction workers were busily building several new homes across the street from the Howard residence. Melvin remembered that that summer had been exceedingly hot and sticky. Roofing a new house and working with hot tar was an undesirable job which the weather made even more miserable. Tom's Kool-Aid stand was an instant hit with the tired, thirsty workers. At first, "The Kool-Aid Kid" as the builders had dubbed Tom, just served cherry Kool-Aid to which he added his own sugar. But, eventually Tom used some of his profits to buy additional flavors and later even instant iced tea. He used Dixie cups and charged a nickel a cup. Since the cups were small, each worker usually bought at least two cups per break. After all the price was reasonable, and furthermore, Tom's product was convenient. Plus, the workers all liked "The Kool-Aid Kid," and they were compelled to give Tom their business. In fact, they were so compelled that Tom raked in a little over one hundred dollars that summer. With that money Tom started his bank account, bought a new bicycle, and paid for he and a friend to go to a Mud Hens baseball game.

Melvin continued breaking twigs and stuffing them into garbage bags, remembering. Remembering how Tom had diligently set the stand up for business each morning at nine o'clock, Monday through Friday. Then, on Saturdays he maturely counted his inventory, made a list, and rode his old bicycle to the local market to replenish his ever-popular stock. At the time Melvin Howard had his son pegged for being the sales or marketing manager for a big company. But, now that idea could be cast aside because despite Melvin's original hopes and dreams Tom had practically no interest in pursuing a college education. For some reason Tom's studies never inspired him the way hard work did. The receiving of the intangible goal of knowledge never seemed to speak to Tom quite as loudly as dollars to be earned.

"Hi, Dad." Tom was coming across the yard now.

"Oh, hi son." Melvin reached down to gather several more small twigs.

"Ready to mow the yard?" Melvin asked once Tom had gotten close enough.

"Oh yeah, I suppose so," Tom said flatly despite the unrelinquishing smile attached to his face that Melvin had just now noticed.

"You look proud of yourself, for some reason," Melvin pried.

"Because I am," Tom began. "I'm nervous, but I'm glad I finally did it."

Melvin quit worrying about the twigs for now to pay better attention to his son.

"Dad, can we talk about something?"

"Sure absolutely."

"Good. I think you'll be proud of me."

To this Melvin felt the faint flame of inspiration begin to grow again inside his soul. Perhaps, after some meticulous thought, the boy had decided to enroll after all in a two year technical school as Melvin had suggested to him just last week.

"Go ahead, son. What is it?" Melvin encouraged.

"First," said Tom. "Let's go inside and sit down. I want Mom to hear this too."

"Sure, Tom. The yard can wait till later, I think."

Once inside the house Melvin successfully interrupted Marcia from preparing a fruit salad so that she could join he and their determined son in the family room. Both Marcia and Melvin assumed their usual chairs while Tom seated himself across from them rigidly on the raised foot of the fireplace, a cool seat for a hot day.

"Mom, Dad, I've made a decision," Tom began slowly. He looked them both in the eyes, and Melvin couldn't help but notice that familiar look of determination in Tom's face. Little did he know that what Tom was about to say would forever change the way Melvin chose to look at the world.

"I know how much the two of you have been concerned about my future now that I've graduated," Tom continued.

Both Marcia and Melvin nodded.

"But, Honey, we don't want to pressure you," Marcia added for assurance.

"That's all right, Mom," Tom said. "The only pressure here, I've placed on myself."

'Bold statement,' thought Melvin and then said, "Go on son. You've got my curiosity."

143

"I've decided to join the Army."

Suddenly the room was quiet. Even though his son sat across from him begging with his eyes for a response, Melvin Howard's tongue had gone lame and speechless. He had hoped for college, instead he got fear. Viet Nam was raging with war and the nightly news never seemed to have anything good to say about how well the Americans were faring over there. Most often, Melvin held Viet Nam synonymous with premature death. Scared, young boys fought a losing battle for what propaganda had convinced them was the security of democracy; yet Melvin could not help but wonder whose democracy these boys were fighting for. Somehow the sacrifice they made was too great.

The room remained quiet for a time more. Tom squeezed his hands nervously and then broke the silence with a slight crack of his knuckles.

"Don't do that, Thomas," said Marcia firmly.

'Odd,' thought Melvin. 'Marcia was a mother one hundred percent of the time.' Knuckles shouldn't matter now, but they did. Everything always did, and now all that mattered to Melvin Howard was that his son was bound for Viet Nam. He possibly would die some bloody, hateful, yet honorable death there in those dreaded jungles, a place where the trees themselves seemed to have rifles, a place where the enemy was seldom seen. 'It was a good thing we always taught him to be careful crossing the street,' thought Melvin absurdly.

"Well?" asked Tom. The silence had to officially end.

Melvin reached for the comfort of Marcia's hand. It was already there, ready to receive his and its comforting squeeze that followed.

"Well, Tom," said Melvin reaching for a pipe and pretending to busy himself with lighting it. "Are you aware of all your options?"

"Dad, the Army will be good for me. When I get out maybe I'll have the discipline to understand why college is so important."

"That's all well and fine, Tom; but what about the War?"

Tom wrung his hands, started to crack his knuckles again, and thought better of it. "Yeah, I know," Tom said.

"I'm scared," Marcia said with her voice shaking. Then, quickly she stood up and hustled to the kitchen choking back her tears.

"Oh Mom!" Tom stood to follow her, but Melvin's firm wave sufficiently re-seated his son.

"I didn't mean to upset her," Tom said.

"I'm sure you didn't, son," said Melvin. "But, you would be lying to yourself if you thought that newsflash would have been received perfectly by both of us. Especially your mother."

"I guess so." Tom was thoughtful and now apparently discouraged. The proud elation that covered his face moments ago was now replaced by concern—the kind of concern that is tainted with guilt.

"Tom, I know you don't want to hurt us," said Melvin. "But, are you thinking about yourself here? Because in this case, that's what is most important."

Tom hung his head and sighed. "Yes sir, I have, completely."

"And?"

"And, I really want to fight for my country. I believe, deep down, that the war effort is really for our own good," said Tom. It didn't matter if his statement sounded like a recruiter's hype speech, Tom Howard was convinced, completely.

"Aren't you afraid?" asked Melvin.

"Well, I suppose so, Dad," said Tom shrugging his shoulders. "But, I really don't know what to be afraid of yet."

"There could be plenty," said Melvin. Suddenly though he wished that he had not said that. He did not want to discourage Tom. What the boy was taking on was after all noble and definitely courageous. Yet, Melvin did not worry any less. He tried to picture Tom in battle fatigues, and his eyes could not envision what his mind refused to let him see. What Melvin did see was the face of a very confused young man searching for a way to appropriately please his father and ultimately please himself. Tom at that moment lived and breathed for Melvin's fatherly blessing. It made no difference how strong Tom's opinions on the subject might actually be. What mattered was for Melvin to simply give the "okay".

"Dad, I'll be careful."

Melvin remembered the boy crossing the street again. He had to face it, here and now. Everyone gets to a point in their lives where they have to cross. Perhaps, this was Tom's crossing.

The room became uncomfortably quiet while both of them thought, considered, and re-considered.

"Just remember, Thomas that it is impossible to make everyone around you happy. This won't be the last time either, but you deserve to make your own choices—however good or bad they might be—because you are the one who must live with these decisions. Make yourself happy first then if there's time make the rest of us happy."

"I love you, Dad," said ever-growing Thomas Howard as he hugged his father again.

XXXI

"Well, Martin," said Melvin Howard picking up the deck of cards and shuffling them. "I did get to see my son again. I was lucky. Plenty of other parents during that time were not so lucky."

"Where is he now?" I asked.

"Oh, Thomas lives in Columbus with his wife. He's been married about four years now. He has a good job in business, and he and his wife are expecting their first baby," said Melvin Howard as if he had rehearsed the information. "Unfortunately his job being what it is, I don't get a chance to see him very often. He gets very busy."

I could tell that Melvin Howard missed his son, and strangely I hoped that some day my father would have a similar reaction to my being away from home.

"Did Tom get hurt in the war?" I asked impulsively.

"Oh yes. Once, only a minor injury," said Melvin Howard. He was driving a jeep through a minefield, I guess, and one of the mines exploded. The jeep was thrown. Tom suffered only a broken ankle in the accident."

I winced any way.

"Well, that was it though," said Melvin Howard. "His ankle was broken bad enough that it required some surgery. He was discharged soon afterward. I guess the ankle still gives him a little trouble."

Then Melvin Howard abruptly changed the subject. "Go to the fair, Martin. Have fun now because everything isn't always fun later. And, I know leaving home isn't one of them. It was hard for me, it was hard for my son, and it will also be difficult for you." He paused. "So, be confident in your decisions since you're really the only one who has to live through them."

As it turned out, Melvin Howard was right. I had a great time with Jason at the State Fair. The two of us rushed right over to Melvin Howard's upon our arrival home to let him in on the good times that we had had.

Throughout the remainder of the summer though I saw Melvin Howard less and less on a social basis. I still worked Saturdays with him, and on Saturdays, we were the best friends ever. But, away from my Saturday work detail, Jason was my best friend. The two friends, however, were different. Melvin Howard was my guidance that I so eagerly sought. Jason was my equal. Jason was somebody I could grow with and share experiences with. I've come now to realize that everyone needs a Jason Forester and everyone could benefit from a Melvin Howard.

Knowing this, I am sure that I was fortunate as an adolescent despite my original lack of acceptance. I had two great friends at a time when true friendships are very important. Because of the support these two people gave me, I became stronger. I also believe I lent each of them something too. I made starting over for Jason a whole lot easier while to Melvin Howard I allowed him the chance to feel needed at a time in his life when very few people expressed a need for him any longer. Caring and nurturing are actually hard habits to break. Through Melvin Howard's friendship, I realized that all of us need to be needed, no matter how silly the reason. We need to feel like we can take someone else less experienced than us under our wing to guide them through the struggles of eventually flying solo.

XXXII

Melvin Howard was right about leaving home. In the next couple years I found that out. It came time to leave for college and through all of Melvin Howard's positive influence it was no great surprise that I selected Ohio Northern University. "Ohio Northern is like a piece of the Ivy League growing in the secure confines of a cornfield," Melvin Howard said, describing the college once when he was helping me sort through the various college pamphlets I had received in the mail. But, even though Ohio Northern was close to familiar scenery, it was nearly a million miles away from everything else. I had to live on campus, an experience that later I decided was quite valuable because of the diversity of people one can meet on a college campus. And, despite my days as a socially outcast seventh grader, I met plenty of people at ONU that I came to know as friends. In addition to relocating, I had to do without Melvin Howard's weekly guidance. I really felt like I was on my own. Honestly I did not always know quite where I was going either. On the day I left I went to see Melvin Howard in the morning.

We both stood on his porch shaking hands for what seemed like a long time. His face glowed warmly like the fire in the hearth during our first meeting. In his eyes I saw my reflection in his pupils briefly, but long enough to know that in his eyes, my confidence had grown.

"Are you all packed," Melvin Howard said, patting my shoulders firmly.

"Yes, all packed."

"How do you feel?"

"Well, I'm nervous," I said.

"That's good," remarked Melvin Howard. "You should be."

"What do you mean? That doesn't sound so good."

"No, Martin, I guess it doesn't sound good at all, does it?" laughed Melvin

148

Howard. "What it does mean," he went on, "is that you should never expect too much or too little. Being nervous insures that, keeps you guessing."

I laughed since I supposed he was right. After all, Melvin Howard had already journeyed down the road that I was just about to navigate.

"Here," he said.

"What is it?" I asked as he held an envelope out to me.

"It's something to get you started."

I looked inside to find a fifty dollar bill staring up at me. "I can't take this."

"Why not?"

"Well, you've done so much for me all these years."

"That's right, and you've done a lot for me too, Martin." Melvin Howard was reliving his life as a parent again, and little did he know, but that single statement prepared me best. It was time to leave.

"Make me proud of you. I'm sure you will," said Melvin Howard.

"Yes, sir." Then we hugged and promised to stay in contact as best as we could.

When I turned to go, I was already flying under my own power. Flying would never be easy, but I knew with all that Melvin Howard had given me, things would be manageable. As I stepped off the porch, I couldn't help but feel the warmth within me. Everything would be all right. Even though I still did not know what I would be facing beyond Melvin Howard's porch at the moment, I knew that somehow I would never really be facing anything alone.

Michael T. Krieger has published several original
poems in national anthologies and has received
awards for his short stories. MELVIN HOWARD'S
FIRESIDE CHATS is his first novel. Michael T.
Krieger resides in Rossford, Ohio where he is a
high school English teacher.